Welcome to Harlequin's great new series,
created by some of our bestselling authors
from Down Under:

THE AUSTRALIANS

Twelve tales of heated romance and adventure—
guaranteed to turn your whole world upside down!

Travel to an Outback cattle station, experience the
glamour of the Gold Coast or visit the bright lights
of Sydney where you'll meet twelve engaging young
women, all feisty and all about to face their biggest
challenge yet...falling in love.

And it will take some very special women to tame
our heroes! Strong, rugged, often infuriating and
always irresistible, they're one hundred percent prime
Australian male: hard to get close to...but even
harder to forget!

The Wonder from Down Under:
where spirited women win the hearts of
Australia's most independent men.

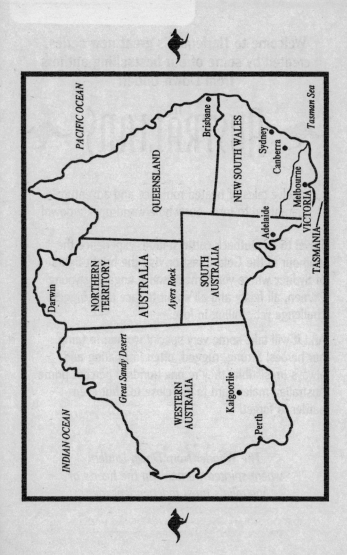

PACIFIC OCEAN

QUEENSLAND

Brisbane

NEW SOUTH WALES

Sydney

Canberra

Tasman Sea

Melbourne

VICTORIA

Adelaide

TASMANIA

NORTHERN TERRITORY

AUSTRALIA

Ayers Rock

SOUTH AUSTRALIA

Darwin

Great Sandy Desert

WESTERN AUSTRALIA

Kalgoorlie

Perth

INDIAN OCEAN

THE AUSTRALIANS

BOOTS IN THE BEDROOM!

Alison Kelly

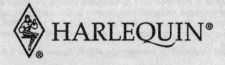

TORONTO • NEW YORK • LONDON
AMSTERDAM • PARIS • SYDNEY • HAMBURG
STOCKHOLM • ATHENS • TOKYO • MILAN • MADRID
PRAGUE • WARSAW • BUDAPEST • AUCKLAND

ISBN 0-373-82581-1

BOOTS IN THE BEDROOM!

First North American Publication 1999.

This edition published by arrangement with Harlequin Books S.A.

® and TM are trademarks of the publisher. Trademarks indicated with ® are registered in the United States Patent and Trademark Office, the Canadian Trade Marks Office and in other countries.

Printed in U.S.A.

Alison Kelly, a self-confessed sports junkie, plays netball, volleyball and touch football, and lives in Australia's Hunter Valley. She has three children and the type of husband women tell their daughters doesn't exist in real life! Not only is he a better cook than Alison, but he isn't afraid of vacuum cleaners, washing machines or supermarkets. Which is just as well; otherwise this book would have been written by a starving woman in a pigsty!

PROLOGUE

'Is it too late to hand in my resignation?' Gina asked, reluctantly moving toward the airport security gate.

'Yes,' her boss returned. 'I told you that when we first discussed this.'

'*We* didn't discuss anything,' Gina corrected. '*You* thrust an airline ticket at me and *told* me I was going.'

'And so you are.' The reed-thin redhead grinned. 'See, it's like I said when I first hired you, I'm the boss so I'm always right.'

Gina refused to smile. 'A fateful day if ever there was one.'

She'd worked for Helen Matherson since two days after she'd graduated second in her class from Sydney University and quickly risen through the ranks at CompuMagic. At twenty-eight she was the firm's senior programmer, answerable only to Helen Matherson, the firm's owner and founder. She was consulted on all staffing matters and new accounts, and if a client requested a personalized computer program she had first shot at it. If she chose not to take on the project, due to either its lack of challenge or her lack of time, it was her responsibility to allocate the job to the person she considered most capable of handling it.

At least that was how things *usually* worked! In this particular instance Helen had neither consulted nor given her a choice, presenting everything as fait accompli the minute Gina had walked into her office the day after returning from a skiing vacation in New Zealand.

My brother wants this done, your flight to Queensland is booked for Sunday, stay as long as it takes to get things running perfectly and don't come back until it is!

With a resigned sigh, Gina dragged her mind to the present and realized Helen was looking at her expectantly. 'What?' She frowned.

'I asked if you have any last-minute questions?'

'Yeah, two. What did I do to deserve this? And couldn't you've just fired me for it?'

'Only an idiot would sack their best programmer, and it's because you're the best that I want you to do this. This might be a family favour, but Parish has promised that if he's satisfied with the program we deliver, he'll steer a lot of new accounts our way. There isn't anyone I'd trust this job to except you, Gina.'

Though it was great to know her boss held her in such high regard, it didn't make Gina any more eager to be part of Sydney airport's Monday morning commuter throng and destined to be heading to the back of beyond. She heartily wished herself a thousand miles away—a thousand miles, that was, in any direction except the one she was headed, a godforsaken hole somewhere in central Queensland.

'Oh, cheer up, for heaven's sake! Think of it as an adventure!' Helen urged as another sigh escaped her lips. 'It's not the end of the world.'

'Not yet, anyway.' Gina had no more desire to experience an adventure in Outback Australia than she did to pour red wine onto the white carpet of her penthouse apartment. Less.

'Here. For the flight.' Her boss shoved three magazines into her hand, *Cosmopolitan*, *Cleo* and *Forum*. She tapped the last with a porcelain fingernail and wiggled her eyebrows. 'Check out the hunk on page fifteen,' she said, sounding more like one of Gina's eighteen-year-old sisters than a forty-one-year-old company executive. 'At ten thousand feet just looking at him will be orgasmic!'

Despite herself, Gina laughed. Helen was utterly incorrigible when it came to men! Unfortunately, though, the announcement of her flight over the P.A. curbed her momentary good humour.

'So much for that pilots' strike I've been praying for,' she muttered. 'What car company did you book the hire—'

The other woman slapped her forehead. 'Oh, hell, I forgot!'

'Gee, thanks, Helen! That's all I need. I'll get there and the only hire car in the whole godforsaken place will be gone!'

'No, no! Gina, darling, I've got *good* news. Instead of having to drive all the way from Mount Isa airport to my brother's, you'll be met by one of his neighbours who's got a private plane. His name is Ron Galbraith, and he'll fly you right to Parish's door. Well, practically the door,' she amended. 'Malagara has an airstrip, and someone will meet you there.'

'Well, Helen, we've vastly different ideas as to what constitutes good news. Mine would've been, "Gina, darling, there's been a change of plans, you don't have to go".'

'Get over it, kid. You're on the plane.' She shook her head. 'Honestly, you'd think I was consigning you to Antarctica instead of a multimillion-dollar property and a nice warm climate.'

'Sure. You'd pitch hell as a nice warm climate if it suited you, Helen.'

'Stop grumbling, it won't be anywhere near as bad as you imagine. I stayed on a cattle station once, and it was just wall to wall with those long rangy, hardworking stockmen types.' She sighed before grinning salaciously. 'There's something subtly sexy about a man sheened in honest blue-collar sweat that gets a sophisticated woman's blood humming. And believe me, Gina, Aussie ringers are about as blue collar as they come!'

'Then I guess I don't appreciate subtlety and I'm not

sophisticated,' Gina returned, picking up her briefcase. 'I like my men sipping champagne and leaving their sweat on my satin sheets, not swilling beer and sweating on the sofa!'

CHAPTER ONE

IT'D BEEN a mongrel of a day. Seventeen hours of heavy manual labour broken up by one small-scale disaster after another.

If there was a part of Parish's body that didn't ache he couldn't distinguish it from those that did. Hard physical labour didn't bother him... No, it was niggly, unexpected problems he didn't have the time to deal with—that really ticked him! And today he'd been constantly ticked from the crack of dawn!

He'd been on his way out to the Tea Party Creek muster yards to repair a section of fence in the branding yard when the new ute he'd been driving had blown a radiator hose. Stupidly assuming a radiator hose would last longer than three weeks, he'd seen no urgency in buying a spare—until today. The oversight had meant hauling Rusty away from his work and sending him a hundred and eighty kilometres into Cloncurry for a replacement. While the whole episode was an irritating start to the day, it faded in comparison to being interrupted in the middle of fencing and told the central bore was mucking up.

That unexpected problem had further thrown his day's schedule into disarray. He'd spent hours he didn't have working on the problem, and though he'd managed to get the bore at least semi-functional, he'd still have to phone Snake and get him up to Malagara a few days early to fix it properly. The central bore was crucial to the second muster, but more so now given the unseasonable heat.

At this stage of The Dry, though the nightly temperature could drop to about seven degrees Celsius, the days were usually a workable twenty-five. Today, by the time Parish

made it back to the branding yards, the mercury had been
hovering in the high thirties, making a miserable job worse.
He'd finished wrestling with fencing wire around five
o'clock, but determined to get his day back on schedule,
he'd wrung the most out of the last shreds of daylight working with the new colt he'd bought. The satisfaction in getting the chore done without any unforeseen interruptions
vanished when the high-strung animal had unloaded him
headfirst into the dirt and bolted. He'd only now secured
the beast in his paddock.

Yep, it'd been a mongrel day, all right!

The creak of the fence gate dividing Malagara's century-
old main house from the other buildings within the homestead compound was loud in the night's silence, and as he'd
been doing for six months, Parish made a mental note to
oil it. It wasn't that he kept forgetting to do it, just that his
mental list of to do's exceeded the time available to get it
done. What with horse breaking, fencing, machinery main-
tenance and preparing for the start of mustering next week,
gate hinges, along with the thousand and one other things
that needed fixing, couldn't get a look-in.

'Damn!' Like that, he thought, cursing as fatigue caused
him to stumble on the gap between the third and fifth step
leading to his veranda.

The weatherboard, iron-roofed house needed more than
its gate oiled and back steps fixed, but unless the walls and
roof fell in, Parish had neither the time nor inclination to
repair anything. In fact, right now he intended to do only
three things—have a cold beer, take a long hot shower and
collapse onto his bed. Anything requiring more physical
exertion could wait until he got up at four-thirty tomorrow.
The law of averages said tomorrow couldn't possibly be as
hellish as today.

He negotiated the pitch darkness of the house until he
reached the refrigerator, its door-activated light glowing
into the basically furnished kitchen for the length of time

it took to extract a beer. Ripping open the can, Parish momentarily considered lighting the fire, the late May coolness warranting having it on overnight, then quickly dismissed the idea as too much hard work. It'd take more than the cold to keep him awake tonight.

Taking a long swallow of beer, he blindly flicked the pull tab toward the sink, already heading to the bathroom before a soft metallic ping confirmed his accurate aim.

Parish felt he'd barely closed his eyes before the alarm clock was urging them open again. He flung his left arm out and shut it off. The ringing continued.

Uttering a string of obscenities, he thumped the top of the clock again. Still it shrilled.

Not until he snatched up the offending instrument, seriously tempted to hurl it into the middle of next week, did he realize it was the damn phone that'd woken him. Squinting at the clock, he groaned. It was only a little after eleven. Cursing, he flung back the covers.

'All right! All right! I'm coming!'

There was only one phone in the old house, and given the time, the coldness and Parish's semi-undressed state, he wasn't in a cheerful mood by the time he stumbled to the kitchen and answered it.

'Dunford!' he barked over the sound of the long-distance pips.

'Parish?'

The sound of his sister's voice marginally decreased his annoyance. '*Helen*? What's—'

'Gina was supposed to phone me when she arrived. She hasn't.'

'*Gina*? Who the devil is—'

'You mean she's not there?' Panic filled the question.

'*Here*? Helen, it's the middle of the night. I don't have the foggiest idea what you're talk—'

'The computer expert you asked me to send up!'

He groaned. With everything else that was going on, the decision to computerize Malagara accounts and stock records was the least of his worries. Especially at this hour. 'It slipped my mind. Sorry, Helen.' He sighed. 'Look, I'm beat. I'll call you tomorrow and we'll work out a good time for her to come.'

'Parish! I just told you. *She should be there now*! She was—'

'Here now?'

'Yes! Parish, are you drunk?'

'Don't I wish,' he muttered around a yawn, trying to drag his sleep-deprived brain up to speed.

'I phoned you over a week ago and said—'

'Yeah, yeah. I remember. Look, Helen, there's no need to panic. Her plane was probably late getting into Isa so she decided to stay there rather than driving up here—'

'She wasn't driving! Some mate of yours from Mount Isa airport rang and said he'd arranged a lift for her with one of your neighbours. Someone called Galbraith or something was going to fly her to Malagara. But Parish, if she's not there yet, where— Oh, my God, they might've crashed!'

'Helen—'

'Those private planes and charters always—'

'Helen!' he cut in more sharply, then drew a long breath to temper his tone. 'Calm down, okay? *They haven't crashed.* A light plane goes down up here and we hear about it. And I'd sure hear if something happened to Ron Galbraith.'

'So where's Gina then? Why isn't she there? Why hasn't she called?'

Only the genuine distress in his sister's voice kept the irritation out of his own. 'Knowing Ron's affinity for socializing and playing the role of wealthy cattle baron, she's probably out at Primrose Downs washing down a five-star meal with hundred-year-old port. Relax. I'll call there and have... What's her name again?'

'Gina. Gina Petrocelli.'

'I thought you were sending some bloke?'

'Yes, well, I decided Elliott was too unreliable.'

'This Gina doesn't sound much of a prize, either, if she doesn't check in with you when she's supposed to.'

A heavy sigh greeted his ear. 'That's what bothers me. Gina *always* checks in. She's one of the most responsible people I've ever met.'

'She probably just forgot and—'

'Don't be ridiculous! Gina doesn't forget things, she's too unflappable for that. I really am worried, Parish.'

'Righto, righto. I'll contact Galbraith's place and have her call you.'

After a few more placating comments to his sister, Parish disconnected the call and expelled a long, tired breath. Lord, all he wanted was to go to bed! But it seemed this miserable day wasn't over yet. Resignedly, he dialled Galbraith's number.

'And then,' Gina said aloud, refusing to acknowledge how dry her mouth was as she paced across the dirt landing strip, hoping motion would defeat the cold, 'after I steal every one of her clients from her, I'm going to buy her company out from under her, assign her to the reception desk and—'

The sound of a car engine halted her plan of revenge on Helen. Heart leaping, she spun in the direction of the noise and a second later had to shield her eyes as a sudden light rose sunlike over the small rise running parallel with the airstrip. Almost instantly two smaller lights followed, and it took a moment before her mind identified the triangular configuration as car headlights and a roof-mounted spot.

'Thank you God! Oh, thank you, thank you, thank you!' she whispered fervently, standing motionless as the vehicle rapidly ate up the dark distance separating them. The driver would either run her down or stop, but both possibilities meant things were looking up.

The four-by-four utility came to a vicious last-minute halt just a few feet from her, and Gina couldn't deny herself the need to reach out and touch it. Through the hood, her fingers absorbed the last vibration of the motor, but as the engine became passive emotional mayhem erupted within Gina. Anger, relief, gratitude and shock all demanded simultaneous release. Of course the relief and gratitude were the Johnny-come-latelies of the bunch. The anger she'd been cultivating for the past five-odd hours was first. Focusing on her anger had been the only way of ignoring how thirsty, hungry and cold she'd become. And she conceded for the first time how afraid she'd been.

'You all right?' a man asked, climbing from behind the wheel.

As he came around to where she stood, two things occurred to Gina. One was that her rescuer was tall, very tall. The other was that, ironically, now, when her safety was assured, she found herself close to tears. Swallowing hard, she fought to keep herself calm, torn between the desire to scream with frustrated rage and throw herself into this strange man's arms and howl like a baby.

'Are you all right?' he repeated.

Not trusting herself to speak, Gina nodded. She tried to smile but couldn't quite pull it off. Under normal circumstances she'd have kept a cautious distance from any strange male, but she'd been alienated from *normal* a lifetime ago. She didn't even bother asking what was in the plastic flask he pushed into her hand. At this point, if it was wet she'd drink it. Her hand trembled with anticipation as she raised the bottle to her lips, thirsty eagerness causing liquid to trickle down her chin. It was cool, familiar and more delicious than the best champagne. *God, had water ever tasted so good?*

During his mad four-kilometre dash from the homestead to the airstrip, Parish had pretty much resigned himself to spending the rest of the night combing the sixty square kilometres of Malagara's bullock paddock searching for an inexperienced city slicker. At the tail end of a day which'd run in direct accordance with Murphy's Law, finding Gina Petrocelli uninjured and exactly where she was supposed to be ought to count as a miracle. Who knew? He might get some sleep yet.

With a relieved sigh, he reached into the front of the ute and clicked on the C.B. 'Go back to bed, Rusty,' he said when his foreman responded. 'She's okay.' Replacing the handset, he turned his attention to the woman. 'At least you had the sense to stay put,' he said, rubbing a weary hand across his neck. 'I wasn't relishing the thought of a full-scale search and rescue after the day I've had.'

'The day you've had?' she gasped, shoving a mane of dark hair off her face. 'The day *you've* had!' Her voice rose as if she was worried he hadn't heard her the first time.

'I've been stranded in this godforsaken spot with nothing to eat or drink since I can't remember when! One minute it's so hot I practically have to strip naked to stay cool, and the next… *the next,*' she fumed, 'it's so damn cold I have to put on God knows how many sweaters plus *this*!'

This to Parish looked like a bathrobe. There appeared to be considerable bulk beneath it, but Parish couldn't guess how much was clothing and how much was her. He had to concede she'd shown good sense in protecting herself against the elements, though judging from the six pieces of luggage sitting a few feet away, she had enough clothes to survive an Antarctic blizzard. Obviously computer experts didn't travel light. Nor did they need to draw breath on a regular basis, because she was still rabbiting on.

'I've fought off flies, mosquitoes and Lord knows what other kinds of bugs! All the time wondering if that herd of ugly cows over there were going to charge me! So *don't* start telling me how bad *your* day's been!'

Parish could've told her that five Brahman heifers wouldn't have constituted a herd even to a Pitt Street farmer, just as he could've told her the cattle in question were being hand-raised by Rusty's kids and wouldn't have stampeded had a bomb gone off next to them. Wisdom told him he'd be wasting his breath. "Yeah, well, if you're ready now, we'll get started for—"

'I've been ready for six hours! Would you mind telling me,' she asked in a superior tone, 'why no one was here to meet my plane?'

'Sorry about that. Seems a few wires got crossed. Everyone thought you were arriving by car. Reckon it's been a mongrel day all round.'

'It's been the day from hell, that's what it's been! And the night's been no picnic, either! I tried phoning the house every ten minutes until I flattened the battery in my mobile!'

He wondered what it'd take to flatten *her* battery. 'Mobiles only work around Isa. No network out here for them yet.'

'No net—' She threw her arms skyward. 'Great! I've landed in the nineteenth century! There's probably no such thing as electricity, much less airconditioning or refrigeration! Nothing but heat, dirt, dust and…and *nothing*!'

Even on a good day Parish didn't have any time for hysterical females, and only the knowledge she was justifiably upset stopped him from telling her to shut up or he'd leave her here for the rest of the night. 'Look,' he said, striving to keep his voice reasonable. 'Why don't you hop in the ute while I get your luggage. I reckon you're looking forward to having a feed and a cuppa.'

'What I'm *really* looking forward to is telling Parish Dunford exactly what I think of his deplorable treatment of visitors! And after that a very long, very hot shower.'

'Well, Miss Petrocelli, one of those ambitions is futile and the other redundant.'

'Why?' She followed him as he picked up two of her bags and deposited them in the back of the ute.

'First, we're fresh out of hot water. And second, *I'm* Parish Dunford.'

'Oh, my God!'

It pleased Parish that she looked totally mortified at learning his identity.

'Oh, my God,' she repeated, lifting a horrified hand to her throat. *'There's no hot water?'*

CHAPTER TWO

'AND then she burst into tears! All because I said she'd have to wait until morning to have a shower!'

It was just past five the following morning, and as usual Parish was having breakfast in the kitchen of his foreman, Rusty Harrington.

'Hell,' he said. 'Take these city women away from their creature comforts for five minutes and they're about as useful as teats on a bull.'

'Oh, Parish, that's not fair!' Leanne Harrington chided. 'Even *I* wouldn't like to spend the night in the middle of the bullock paddock all alone. The thought of a nice relaxing shower at the end of it all was probably the one thing that stopped her falling apart out there. And after the day she'd spent, it's only natural she'd be a bit emotionally fragile.'

'Yeah? Well, there was nothing fragile about the way she ripped into Helen when she got on the phone to her. *Or,*' he said, reaching for the teapot and pouring himself another cup of tea, 'the language she used when she tripped on the back steps and spread-eagled herself on the veranda.'

'Just *forgot* to warn her about that step, eh, Parish?' Rusty's casual question came with a speculatively amused gleam in his eye.

Parish grunted. 'It was a genuine oversight. I was so tired I tripped on the damn thing myself earlier. Although...' He smiled. 'I'll admit a certain amount of satisfaction at seeing her momentarily left speechless.'

Not that it'd lasted long, he recalled. Almost immediately she'd started muttering about how in the city public safety laws demanded houses in better condition than his be listed for demolition!

'All I hope,' he said, 'is that Gina Petrocelli is half as sharp with computers as she is with her mouth. That way she'll be gone before we're back from the first muster.'

'Well, *I'm* looking forward to having another woman around the place for a while,' Leanne said, awkwardly lowering her pregnant frame onto the chair at the end of the table. 'How old is she?'

Parish was surprised to realize he hadn't paid much attention to her looks, but then again, he'd barely been able to keep his eyes open, much less focus with them, and it'd been her prickly citified attitude that had made the lasting impression. What came to mind when he tried to visualize her was the image of an average-sized, average-looking brunette and an oversized mouth wearing a pricey-looking dressing-gown. It was possible she'd had a cute nose, but it'd been stuck too far in the air for him to tell for certain!

'Parish?'

He looked up to find Leanne giving him the same look her twelve-year-old daughter did when he didn't recognize the name of her latest rock idol.

'Yeah?'

'How old is she?'

'Oh…round thirty, I guess.'

Leanne gave a satisfied nod. 'Good. We'll have things in common to talk about.'

'I doubt it,' Parish muttered under his breath. What little he'd seen of Gina Petrocelli didn't have him drawing favourable comparisons between her waspish, stuck-up attitude and Leanne's friendly, relaxed nature.

Getting to his feet, he carried his plates to the sink. As always, two small coolers sat on the bench, further reason to make him doubt his friend would find much common ground with the recently arrived computer expert. Despite Rusty and Parish's countless protests that they could feed themselves, Leanne was up before the birds to not just serve up a hot breakfast, but to pack lunches for them both, as well. On the other hand, Miss Petrocelli's parting words as she'd taken herself off to his spare bedroom last night had been, *'Usually I'm an early riser and up by seven-thirty, but don't bother fixing breakfast for me in the morning. Tomorrow, I'll probably sleep late.'*

Parish was so stunned by the offhand remark, she'd left the room before he had a chance to tell her seven-thirty was hours past early, and *bulls would produce milk before he'd be fixing her breakfast*! A point he intended making very clear to her at the first opportunity.

Yep, the way he saw it, Gina Petrocelli, with her superior, city-slicker attitude, had less in common with Leanne than ducks did with horses!

She woke up feeling dazed and disoriented, not because she didn't immediately recognize where she was, but because she did. Gina wondered what heinous crimes she'd committed in her past life to be punished so in this one.

The room's stark utilitarianism, glimpsed last night in the glow of the bare two-watt light globe hanging from the ceiling, wasn't enhanced any by the bright sunlight streaming through the dirt-streaked window. A mirrorless single wardrobe and a chest of drawers broke the monotony of the three-metre wall opposite the one her cast-iron bed was shoved against, and in perfect alignment to the window on the wall to her left was the door on her right. Beside the bed, jarring with the thoroughly Amish decor of the rest of the room, was a sixties style aqua vinyl armchair.

Even more depressing than her Spartan surroundings was the knowledge that beyond the door, things weren't any better. In fact, considering she'd have to face Parish Dunford again, she could understand why dying in one's sleep held such appeal for some people. Not that Gina had given much thought to how she'd like to die until yesterday, when it had looked as if she was destined to perish on some isolated Outback airstrip. Now wouldn't *that* have wrecked poor Parish Dunford's already mongrel day? And imagine how put out he'd have been, having to take time off to attend an inquest and explain how an unfortunate computer programmer had come to die of exposure on his property. It'd be worth being dead just to inconvenience him!

She groaned. Gee, she really was in a bad way if the only bright side to the whole sorry situation was the thought of her own demise! But she couldn't help it. Being out here reminded her too much of a part of her life she'd fought hard to forget.

After a few more minutes lying there wallowing in self-pity and day-old dust, grime and sweat, Gina decided her lot wouldn't get any better without positive action on her part. If she wanted out of this place she was first going to have to get out of bed! Dunford had promised there'd be hot water this morning.

Oh, God, she couldn't believe she'd cried like that!

She'd often wondered what her breaking point was, and now she knew. Never again was she going to let anyone she couldn't sue make transport arrangements for her! Helen made a terrific boss...well, up until this deal with her brother she'd made a terrific boss.

Her mind having drifted to the reason she was here, Gina kicked back the bedding. The sooner she had a shower and dressed, the sooner she could start work on the program. The sooner she started it, the sooner she'd finish it and be on her way back to Sydney. And the sooner she got back to Sydney the better!

What sounded fine in theory didn't always translate well into practise, Gina conceded an hour later, when, after going through every room in the house, she still hadn't located a computer. Heck, she hadn't seen anything that looked like it had come into existence since 1960. Standing on the veranda, she squinted against the glare as she visually checked out the other buildings she could see from the house. Last night she'd paid them little or no attention. There were three large aluminium hangar-type constructions, which she presumed were sheds or workshops of some kind, which could feasibly contain an office, but it was the unexpected sight of a modern brick house only a few hundred metres away that drew her curiosity.

Basic and modest in design, with landscaping that consisted of a few random tufts of grass in a sea of dusty ground, it was exactly the sort of country homestead she'd expected to find herself staying in on this trip, something rural but comfortable. *So much for harbouring mediocre expectations, Gina, my girl!* she thought. Compared to the accommodation she'd ended up with, the other place was positively palatial. *I'll bet they've got a shower that delivers more than three drops of water at a time.*

Head down, Gina carefully made her way over the uneven ground towards the house. It occurred to her she should've taken the time to get her sunglasses—the glare up here was blinding! It was also becoming increasingly obvious that the wardrobe she'd packed wasn't as practical for this particular assignment as it had been for past on-site jobs. Three-inch heels and beige silk somehow didn't seem to deliver the wearer the same cool confidence crossing a dusty yard in the Outback as they did crossing foam-backed carpet in an airconditioned office. The instant she made the silent comparison her foot hit a small hole. She swore.

'I see your vocabulary hasn't improved any with all that sleep. Guess you need more than fourteen hours.'

The male voice from her nightmare of the previous day came just as she was regaining her balance. She straightened with what she hoped passed as poise and found herself eye to *chest* with the man. When she tilted her head, she met amused blue eyes.

'I've been up for nearly two hours, Mr Dunford. Most

of which I've spent searching for a computer I still haven't found.'

'Well, look on the bright side, at least you found the shower. That seemed to be your biggest priority last night.' There was a smirk on his mouth as his eyes looked her up and down. 'We'd both had a rough day, which explains why neither of us was in any condition to focus on details then.'

He shifted his stance and shoved his hat back, the action drawing attention to his tall, perfectly proportioned physique and revealing a rugged handsomeness she hadn't expected. Gina conceded that, had she met him dressed in a suit at a dinner party or business meeting, she'd have been checking out the third finger of his left hand before she'd finished shaking his right. That it had taken her until now to question Parish Dunford's marital status, however, proved she was objective when it came to good looks and well-toned body. She could appreciate a broad male chest and long muscular legs poured into snug worn denim just as much as the next woman, but fortunately her early encounters with blue-collar Australian males had immunized her against their raw sex appeal and rough-edged charm.

'Well,' he drawled. 'I'm sure if you stand there thinking hard enough about where that computer is, it'll come to you.'

Gina almost blurted it wasn't the computer she'd been musing about, but fortunately he started to stride away before she blundered. The view of him walking away was engaging to the mind, too, and—

'Oh, by the way!' he added.

Gina hastily lifted her eyes from his butt.

'Don't take what I'm going to say the wrong way,' he went on. 'But…well, the thing is, you're not really dressed for being out here.'

Like she needed him to tell her that!

'You keep running round without a hat and you're gonna fry.'

'A hat.'

'Yep.' Parish kept his voice deadpan. 'Sunscreen's a waste of time. Only sweats right off as soon as you put it on. There's a few spare hats hanging on the back of the kitchen door. One of them should fit you.' He waved a hand to a fenced-off bit of dirt. 'I'll be over in the breaking yard if you need me. Good luck finding that computer.'

He might have a body to die for, but the guy was already brain dead, Gina decided.

'Mr Dunford!' she called.

'It's Parish.' He tossed the words over his shoulder.

'Fine! Parish,' she agreed, hurrying to catch up with him once she realized he wasn't going to stop. 'It'd save time if you just told me where it was.'

He stopped abruptly, causing her to almost collide with him. 'Where what is?' He frowned.

Give me strength! she thought. 'The computer,' she said aloud.

He shrugged. 'Well, I figure it's in one of those cases I lugged inside. If not, perhaps you left it on Ron's—'

'I don't mean I can't find my laptop!' she snapped. 'Of course, that's in my luggage. Where's *your* computer? The one I'm suppose to program.'

If possible, his expression grew even more blank. 'You mean you've lost it?'

'Lost it! I've never found it! I don't have the—'

Now it was Parish who turned the air blue. 'Are you telling me you didn't bring one up here with you?'

'Bring it—' Realization was painful. 'You mean you don't even *have* a computer?'

'Of course I don't have a computer! If I already had a computer I wouldn't have had Helen going on and on about installing one for me! That's what I thought she was sending you here to do!'

'It is!' Gina said, raising her voice so he wouldn't think he'd cornered the market on irritation. 'At least I'm supposed to set up a personalized program for you. I assumed you already *had* the hardware. Had the *computer*,' she expanded when he frowned. 'I'm a software specialist. Usually the hardware is already in place by the time I take on a job.'

Parish looked skyward and muttered under his breath before bringing his gaze to Gina.

'Are you saying—' his words came out with the exaggerated slowness people use when they're reining in their anger or speaking with an idiot or both '—that you don't know enough about computers to be able to drive to Mount Isa, buy one and set it up?'

'Don't be ridiculous! Of course I know that!'

'Good. Then problem solved,' he said. 'You'll take the ute, go into Isa and buy whatever you damn well think you need.'

Gina opened her mouth but couldn't decide what words she should force out first. 'Drop dead!... I don't take orders from you!... Which direction is Mount Isa?...or How the hell can I be standing here thinking an arrogant jerk like you is sexy?'

Parish didn't know what was going through her head, but the way her lush little mouth was silently working was causing some pretty risqué thoughts to run through his. Which raised the question of whether he should be going into Isa, too, because if last night he'd seen her as only average-looking, he sure as hell needed to get his night vision checked out!

'If it's all the same with you,' she said finally, 'I'd rather phone Helen and have her send up a top of the range Pentium. It'll probably take a day or two, but at least that way I know I'll get exactly what I need.'

'Whatever. I don't have the foggiest idea what a Pentium is, so I guess I'll just have to trust Helen's assessment that you're good when it comes to finding your way around a computer.' He smiled. 'That is, when you can find one.'

A wry smile nicked her mouth as she raised a perfectly arched eyebrow. 'I'll give you a tip, Parish. In the last few days I've found that trusting your sister isn't always in one's best interests, least of all when it comes to travel arrangements. But rest assured, I'm *very* good at what I do.'

'And does that apply to *everything* you do...or just your work?'

Though her pulse skittered at the suggestive laziness of his voice and sweeping gaze, Gina schooled her tone to coolness. 'Both. But here's another tip—if you're trying to hit on me, you're wasting your breath. You're not my type.'

'I see.' He grinned with obvious amusement. 'In other words you prefer city slicks over country hicks.'

'Since you're being so blunt,' she said, wondering what the hell she had to feel embarrassed about, 'Exactly! I prefer my men cultured and sophisticated!'

He gave her such a patronizing smile, she wanted to slap it off his damned face.

'Relax, Gina. When I decide to hit on a woman, I don't leave them in doubt as to what's happening. Besides, you're not my type, either.' He shook his head, once more looking at her clothes. 'You've got lousy dress sense.'

CHAPTER THREE

'HEY, Parish! How many fingers am I holding up?'

At the sound of Rusty's voice, Parish stepped back from the horse he was unsaddling and watched his friend's approach. Both Rusty's hands were hooked into his belt. 'This another one of the jokes the kids brought home from school?'

'Nope, it's an eyesight test,' Rusty said seriously. 'You told me she was *average*.'

'So I exaggerated.'

'Very funny! Mate, she's a knockout!'

Shrugging, Parish returned his attention to the horse.

'Aw, pull the other one, Dunford! She's a stunner, and you say otherwise and you're either a liar or an idiot. And you've never been a liar.'

'Not about to start being an idiot, either. I won't deny Gina Petrocelli is a looker, but God would've done the male race a bigger favour if he'd understated her figure and ego a bit more and invested the difference in her humility.' Lifting the saddle, he headed to the tack room. 'That city slicker is so far up herself she doesn't need a bloke!'

Rusty let loose a loud howl. 'She knocked you back!'

'Knocked me back? Ha! Mate, she didn't even wait to be asked! I got shot on suspicion.' He didn't say the suspicion was justified, but the admission drew more raucous laughter from his burly friend.

'Thanks for your support on this, Rus.'

'Sorry, mate.' Rusty was still shaking with mirth.

'I take it if you've seen Gina you've been up at the house. Let me guess.' Parish theatrically put his fingers to his temples. 'Leanne wanted you to ask Gina to dinner.'

'Yep. Guess that proves you haven't lost *all* your perception where women are concerned.'

'Leanne's slipping. I'd have backed her to have had her over for lunch. Course, lunch might've been a bit early in the day for some people,' he muttered, before realizing all good humour had disappeared from the other man's face.

'Rusty? What's wrong?'

The burly redhead shook his head. 'Oh, probably nothing, but…'

'But?'

'Well, she hasn't said anything, Lee wouldn't, you know… But, well, I think this pregnancy's knocking her about more than the others did.' He sighed. 'Hell, it's probably just this damn heat! Makes everyone feel punch-drunk.'

Having known this man for fifteen years, Parish immediately recognized his concern went deeper than he was letting on.

Their friendship had started when Rusty signed on as a ringer at Dunford Downs, Parish's grandfather's property. At seventeen, the runaway Rusty immediately became an idol to the rebellious fourteen-year-old Parish. Though their friendship had all the ingredients for disaster, strangely, the arrival of the other boy into his then turbulent life had a stabilizing effect on Parish. Four years later, when Parish, with his grandfather's blessing, decided to try his hand mustering on the vast cattle stations of the Territory and Far North Queensland, Rusty was with him.

It was just a few months later, while they were working in the Gulf country, they met Leanne. Parish had teasingly told her she had the prettiest seat he'd ever seen on a stockman, but she never heard him. Her eyes lit up the minute she caught sight of Rusty Harrington. Twelve years and five kids later, the glow was still there, but now it was the concerned look in Rusty's eyes that had Parish's attention.

'When's she due again?' Parish asked quietly.

'Early September. More than three months away.'

'Any chance she'll go early?'

Rusty shook his head, then shrugged. 'She reckons not. Says all the others were at least a week overdue and that if things run to schedule, she'll see out the mustering.'

'Yeah, right. When was the last time things ran to schedule round here?'

Rusty's mouth stretched to a wry smile. 'Gotta be a first time.'

'Don't count on it.' He sighed, realizing that was the last thing Rusty needed to hear. 'Listen, Snake'll be here in a day or two, and between us we'll be able to hold the fort. Why don't you take a week off and take Lee and the kids south. The Downs is close to Rockhampton and—' He broke off at his friend's shaking head.

'We both know there's no way, short of her going into labour, she'll let me ship her out at the start of our first muster on Malagara. For the first time in our lives we've got a personal financial stake in something, and she's so damned excited about it, I'll probably have to chain her to the clothes line to keep her away from the camps!'

Parish smiled. Leanne wasn't the only one who'd been thrilled when, after closing the deal on the purchase of the property last year, he'd offered the pair a ten percent share in it.

'Never mind all that. Leanne's health takes priority over the damn muster.'

'Huh! Only if you're not Leanne. The woman's part Irish, part mule. Aw, hell, Parish, I'm probably worrying about nothin' anyway,' he went on, and Parish wondered which of them he was trying to convince. 'She hasn't complained about feelin' crook or anything.'

'Leanne wouldn't admit to being crook if they had her on life support!'

'Maybe, but she'll be ticked off if she thinks we're pampering her, and you know it. I swear if she says, "I'm having a baby not terminally ill!'' one more time, I'll gag her.'

After six pregnancies, Rusty did a fair imitation of Leanne's favourite response to suggestions she rest or take things easy, and it drew a smile.

'I'm not sure that gagging and roping a pregnant mother to a clothes line will get you a new-age father award,' he said. 'But…okay. We'll let things ride for the time being, but you've got to swear you'll sing out the minute you think things are—'

'Getting too much for her. I'll tell you,' Rusty finished.

'Right. She can kick up as big a stink as she likes, but if necessary, we'll get her out of here if I have to put her on a cattle train to do it.'

For a few moments talk turned to the ringers they'd signed up for the muster, then Rusty announced he was heading home. He was at the door when he looked back and said, 'Oh, by the way, Parish, when Miss Average asked how we dressed for dinner, I told her tonight was casual.' He grinned. 'Thought you oughta know in case you were thinkin' of putting on a tux or somethin'!'

'Get outta here, you smart ass!'

Fifteen minutes later Parish walked into his kitchen to find his visitor concluding a telephone call and decided Gina Petrocelli wouldn't know *casual* if it bit her on the rump!

She wore an ankle-length swirly cream dress with long sleeves and a high neck, and on her feet were a pair of short, spiky-heeled boots that no sane person'd walk in for a bet! Gold hoop earrings hung from her ears, and a chunky bracelet rattled as she hung up the telephone. Parish figured loose, shoulder-length hair was her sole concession to *casual*.

When he strode past her to the refrigerator, she reacted as if expecting him to attack her on sight. Which meant she thought herself irresistible to men, or she thought *he* was a slow learner. She was about to discover she was wrong on both counts!

'I've arranged with Helen to have a computer sent up,' she said.

'Wished you told me before you hung up, I wanted a word with her,' he said.

'Oh, no...*that* was my sister. I wanted her to—' Gina broke off, deciding he didn't need to know she'd asked Sara to send up some more clothes for her. No dress sense, indeed! '...to, um, forward my mail.'

'Want a beer?'

The curt offer came *after* he'd already shut the fridge and propelled the top of his can into the sink.

'No, thank you,' she said with pointed politeness. 'I don't drink beer.'

'That's what I figured.' A smug expression crossed his face as he propped himself against what looked like a twenty-year-old refrigerator. 'Well, the bad news is we're fresh out of champagne, but there should be a bottle of Scotch in that cupboard.' He gestured with a hand without once taking his eyes from her face. 'If not there's a case of it in the main store. Rum, too. Feel free to help yourself.'

He was close enough for Gina to see the slight sheen of perspiration glazing the skin exposed at his throat. His shirt was dirt streaked and damp in patches, and he carried the scent of labour, leather and masculinity. It wasn't until he lifted the beer to his mouth and took a long, lengthy swallow that she remembered men like him were offensive to her.

'Thanks all the same, but I'll pass on the drink,' she said, stepping back. 'Oh, and I won't be here for dinner, either, so there's no need to prepare anything for me.'

She jumped when he made a loud gagging sound, doubled over and started choking. Instinctively she thumped his back. He pushed her away, still choking, before straightening to glare at her through slightly watering eyes. Shiny wet, they looked like cobalt silk.

'I—' He broke off, coughing again. 'Lady,' he managed eventually, the word a gasp. 'If you're expecting me to cook for you, you're going to starve real fast. This isn't one of those tourist cattle stations, this is a working operation, and you're here to work.'

Gina opened her mouth to speak, but didn't get the chance.

'Come next week I'll be gone days on end mustering, and there's not a chance in hell I'm going to hire a cook to keep you fed and watered while I'm away!' he told her. 'Now since we aren't on a takeaway pizza route out here, I suggest you start boning up on how a *manual* can-opener works and check out the canned foods down in the station store. Get the message?'

'If the message is you're the most obnoxious man God ever put breath into, then you're about twenty-four hours late delivering it! I worked that out on my own! For your information I'm more than capable of cooking for myself! In fact, I've single-handedly catered dinner parties for twenty people!'

She had the satisfaction of seeing momentary surprise register in his face, but it vanished quickly.

'Good! Because I don't want you taking advantage of Leanne's generosity while you're here. She's got enough to deal with as it is.'

'Excuse me?'

He snatched off his hat and raked his fingers through his hair, all the time muttering through his teeth. No doubt his words were directed to or about her, but Gina didn't hear them. It was the first time she'd seem him without the battered black Akubra and was amazed to discover that, as blue as his eyes were, his hair was jet black and fashionably cut. In another world and with the aid of a personality transplant, the guy would've been drop dead gorgeous.

'Look,' he said in such a reasonable voice she almost didn't think he was addressing her. 'I know Leanne sent Rusty up to ask you to dinner tonight, but knowing her she'll be inviting you over there to eat every night. Frankly she doesn't need the extra work right now.'

He made it sound like she had the appetite of a bull elephant.

'So you want me to decline the invitation, is that it?'

'Heck, no, not tonight!' He looked aghast. 'Lee's been looking forward to meeting you, but if she suggests you eat there on a regular basis then—'

'*Then* I should decline, because preparing a plate of food for someone with my voracious appetite will send her to an early grave.'

Amusement played at the edge of his mouth a moment before a slow grin slid over his face. 'I'm not in any position to know exactly how voracious your appetite is, Gina.'

'And you never will be!' She pounced on his innuendo.

'Oh, I think I'll have a fair idea after tonight.'

'In your dreams.'

His blue eyes pinned to her, he nonchalantly spun his hat around his finger. 'If we're sharing a dinner table it's going to be hard to keep from noticing things like that.'

'Sharing a— What on earth are you talking about?'

'Why, your appetite for food.' He wore the devil's smirk. 'Weren't you?'

No, it wasn't the devil's smirk he wore, it was the one Satan *borrowed from him* when he needed to be truly odious! Gina was so furious with herself for rising to his bait, she thought she would spontaneously self-combust.

With lazy grace he straightened, crushing the beer can in one hand. 'Well, I'll just take a quick shower,' he said. 'Since we're both going over to Rusty's for dinner, we may as well walk across together.'

'I'm more than capable of finding my way there on my own.'

'True. But I want you to wait for me anyway.'

'Why? Afraid of the dark, are you, Parish?'

'Nope. Afraid of unsuspecting city slickers stepping on a snake and getting bitten,' he said matter of factly. 'Snakes get active at dusk, and the ones up here aren't real sociable.'

Gina stared straight at him. 'So I've noticed.'

'Still,' he said, looking thoughtfully at her feet, her insult rolling off him. 'Those boots are probably sturdy enough to stop a set of fangs doing too much damage,' he said thoughtfully. 'I reckon, if you stay alert, you shouldn't come to any harm. We keep an antivenin on hand. Not allergic to it, are you?'

Again his hundred-watt smirk appeared. *If those teeth are natural, I'm a blonde*! Gina thought.

'Not that I know of.'

'Then I guess there's no reason for you to wait, then.'

'On second thoughts... Considering what I paid for these shoes, I think I will wait for you, after all.' She produced a sickly sweet smile. 'That way if there are any *other* snakes about, they'll see me with you and assume I'm not prejudiced towards reptilian life form.'

His laughter carried to her after he'd left the room, and much to her annoyance Gina found she enjoyed not just the sound, but the sparring that had led up to it. Parish Dunford's dry sense of humour both challenged and appealed to her, and while she didn't deliberately want to dislike him, she certainly couldn't afford to let her guard down around him. Hereditarily, she was cursed with a weakness for rugged, charming, blue-collar Australian males, but she was determined to prove that it was environment, not genetic make-up that most influenced people's behaviour.

And it was definitely this alien environment that was making her so edgy now—*not* Parish Dunford!

At a loss as to what to do until he was ready to leave, she picked up one of the dozen or so magazines piled on the scarred coffee table, used it to brush a fine layer of dust from the vinyl sofa and with a fleeting, resigned glance at her light-coloured dress, sat down. Once she got the computer set up, she'd have to sit down and discuss with Parish exactly what he needed a program to do, but until then reading some of these graziers' magazines might give her a rough idea.

She was only halfway through an editorial on beef export criteria when movement behind her alerted her that Parish had come back into the room. The timber floor creaked as he covered the distance from the doorway to the couch, and she couldn't help noticing his stride sounded as self-assured as it looked. *Not that I'd paid undue attention to either his legs or how he moved*! she reassured herself. Of course some women might argue that Parish's long, muscular legs were due a lot of attention, be they clad in denim or moleskins as they were now, braced apart and directly in her line of vision. She wasn't one of them. Stubbornly she kept her head down.

'I just had a cold shower.'

'Mmmm,' she said, wishing he'd move so she could stand up. He was so close if she uncrossed her knees she'd kick him.

'*I repeat*,' he said tightly. 'I just had a *cold* shower.'

'How macho,' she said flatly. 'I'm impressed.' Her head snapped up as the magazine was snatched from her grasp. 'Wha— You rude—'

'How many showers did you have today?' There was no amusement in the freshly shaved face.

'That's none of your damn business.'

'It is when you selfishly waste all the hot water!' he snarled.

She leapt to her feet. 'I did not selfishly waste anything! I'm entitled to shower any time I want to—and I will!'

'Not while you're here, you won't.'

'I beg your—'

'That tank takes almost six hours to heat and holds only enough for *one* hot shower at a time.'

'Well, I only take one shower at a time! The system's inadequacies are hardly my fault—it's *your* tank.'

'Which is why I expect to get some use out of it.' He stepped forward, his nearness forcing her up against the sofa.

'I do anything from twelve to eighteen hours of work a day, hard, physical, dirty, sweaty work.'

His words invoked a disturbing image of how he'd looked and smelled when he'd come in a little while ago. What made it disturbing was that Gina didn't find it as revolting as he was painting it. And she should have!

'At the end of every day,' he went on, blue eyes glaring, 'there are two things I look forward to...a beer and a shower. I like to take that shower within an hour of knocking off work. So in future, Ms Petrocelli, I expect there to be a full tank of hot water available for me. Which means *you* can't take a shower for six hours before or after I get home.'

'Hey, I have to shower, too—'

'Do it in the morning.'

'And what if I need to take a second one?'

He grinned. 'Well, then, I guess it's the lesser of two evils. Have a cold one...or share a hot one with me.'

'I'd rather bath in a horse trough!'

He snapped his fingers. 'You're right. You have *three* alternatives.'

CHAPTER FOUR

THE Harrington house was a shock to Gina's system. Furnished in mass-produced modern pine furniture and pastels, its only real colour came from five loud but happy children with the too cute names of Kylee, Kaylee, Karlee, Kellee and Billy. Ranging in age from twelve years to thirteen months, their antics would've appealed to only the most maternal of women or the criminally insane.

'Usually we all eat together,' Leanne Harrington told Gina as the four adults sat down at the table. 'But our mob can be a bit rowdy on first meeting so I thought it'd be better to feed the kids first and get them settled down.'

Gina smiled at the tiny, very pregnant, very fatigued-looking blonde. 'You only made extra work for yourself. I wouldn't have minded eating with the children.'

Compared to most of her career-oriented friends, Gina considered herself broad-minded when it came to children. In fact on one or two occasions she'd even speculated that at some point in the future she might *actually have one*! However, after an hour of the Harrington children's boisterous one-upmanship, she decided the model she wanted wasn't going to come from the K series.

'The five of them must be a handful for you,' she went on. 'Even when you *aren't* pregnant.'

'It's easier when school's in and the oldest three are gone most of the day, but...' She shrugged, a smile emphasising the network of fine lines on her make-up free face. 'What can I say, Rusty wanted a big family.'

Gina looked at the cheerful redheaded man to her left. Obviously Rusty was pleased he'd got what he wanted, but the dark lines under Leanne's pretty green eyes said she'd absorbed most of the shrapnel wounds of parenthood. Unfortunately the women always did.

'Both Leanne and me are only children,' he said. 'We didn't want our kids goin' through the boredom and loneliness we did.'

'Being an only child's a bitch all right.' Parish endorsed, causing Gina's head to swing to him.

'How would you know?' she asked. 'You've got what...three or four brothers plus Helen.'

'I've got three stepbrothers and one stepsister.' His tone suggested he enjoyed being able to put her in the wrong...again.

'Oh, I see. I've only ever known Helen by her married name, so I assumed her maiden one was Dunford... Still, that explains it.' Nodding sagely, she returned her attention to her plate.

'Explains *what*?' he asked, as she'd known he would.

'Huh?' she said, feigning momentary vagueness. 'Oh...I was puzzled about how it was you came to have a sister as charming as Helen.'

A wry smile tugged his mouth. 'I don't think *charming* was the word you used to describe her last night.'

'Probably not,' she agreed. 'But then until I met the Harrington family, nothing I'd encountered here reminded me the word was in my vocabulary.'

As their hosts erupted into loud laughter, Parish's blue eyes dropped to her mouth. 'You know,' he whispered, 'given a chance I'd probably develop a real taste for that sharp little tongue of yours.'

Gina's stomach dropped to her toes. Completely bamboozled by the images and sensations he'd triggered within her, it took her a few moments to realize the laughter had died and everyone was looking expectantly at her.

'I'm sorry. What did you say?' She directed the question to Leanne.

'Rus wanted to know if you had brothers an' sisters,' Leanne said, frowning.

'Three younger sisters,' she said quickly, scrambling to pull herself together. 'No brothers. I'm the oldest.'

'That must be on account of only having younger sisters and no brothers, huh?' Parish's expression was droll.

Determinedly she mirrored it. 'Quite possibly.' Averting her gaze, she spoke to the other couple. 'Sara and Emma are the youngest. They're eighteen-year-old twins. My other sister, Carmen, is twenty-one. Her little girl, Liberty, is the same age as Billy.'

'Liberty?' Rusty echoed. 'Weird name to give a kid.'

Gina refrained from asking if that was because it didn't have *lee* tacked to the end of it. 'Carmen is big on individuality and civil liberties. Hence the name. Everyone shortens it to Libby.'

The conversation drifted to potential names for the Harringtons' sixth child. According to Rusty, they'd narrowed it down to Bradley for a boy but hadn't come up with a girl's name yet, because they thought both Karalee and Kyralee would be too easily confused with one of the other girls' names! Gina almost did herself an injury trying to keep a straight face.

Mercifully this conversation was short-lived, and to Gina's surprise she found herself strangely fascinated by the images conjured up by Rusty's humorous anecdotes of life as a stockman. He was a born storyteller, and listening to his colourful turn of phrase and slow drawl was like being drawn into a Banjo Paterson poem. The stories revealed the relationship between Parish and Rusty Harrington went back along way. She was curious about the subtle differences in the speech patterns of the two men, and she puzzled over it.

Parish referred to their meal as *dinner*, as she did, whereas their host said *tea*. Early in the evening Gina had found herself biting her tongue to avoid *rudely* correcting

Rusty's grammar. But Parish's, she noted, was faultless. Though both men spoke in the same unhurried, lazy drawl typical of what city people called *bushies*, there was an educated eloquence in Parish's speech not evident in Rusty's or Leanne's.

As the night drew to an end, Gina couldn't deny it'd been a pleasant and entertaining evening and she'd enjoyed herself immensely. The Harringtons were great company even if what she'd heard and witnessed of Leanne's lifestyle reinforced her intentions not to let her heart rule her head when she decided to marry. Watching the poor woman constantly excusing herself to bring in the next course or attend to some need of the children's while her husband obliviously remained seated burned her up! And while she could comprehend the politeness that made Leanne decline her offers of help, it had been a real fight to keep from saying to the other woman's good-natured husband, '*Hey, Rusty, guess what—fathers are parents, too!*'

Having refilled her husband's teacup and stirred in sugar, as well, Leanne quickly gulped down her own tea, which had gone cold while she'd tucked the younger kids in bed, and began clearing the table. Since Rusty gave no indication he was suddenly going to get off his well-fed backside and help, Gina rose and reached for Parish's empty plate. He looked at her as if she'd taken his wallet.

'Sit down, Gina.' Leanne's command managed to do what Gina herself hadn't been able to—drag her eyes away from Parish's blue ones.

'Don't be silly,' she said. 'I'll help you. You haven't stopped waiting on us all night.'

'Help me tomorrow night when you're a regular. Tonight you're a guest.'

Gina shook her head. 'Thanks, anyway, but I wouldn't dream of intruding on you tomorrow night. You've got more than enough to do now.'

'Exactly. One more won't make a bit of difference,' the

other woman said pleasantly, then smiled. 'Specially one
who eats as little as you. Honestly, Gina, I don't know what
I envy most, your slim figure or the fact you can see your
toes when you stand!'

Parish got to his feet, his shoulder brushing against
Gina's with the action. His calloused fingers sent little electric shocks through her as he took the plates from her
hands. Feeling crowded, she edged to her left where she
could draw more oxygen, laughing to override her awk-
wardness.

'I'm not sure how long I would be seeing my toes if I
ate here regularly, Leanne.'

'She'll be having dinner up at the house,' Parish said.

'Eh?' Rusty said. 'Come again?'

'Rusty.' Gina smiled. 'I've very much enjoyed tonight,
but I'm not going make extra work for your wife when I
can just as easily eat dinner with Parish.'

'We aren't married—'

'Parish always eats here—'

Gina blinked. Normally she might've questioned why a
couple who were committed enough to having five children
hadn't formalized their arrangement and married somewhere along the line. But she had a more important question.

'What do you mean, Parish always eats here?'

'Just that,' Leanne responded, frowning. 'Parish always
has dinner with us. Don't you, Parish?'

Gina swung to face the man who'd warned her against
taking advantage of Leanne's generous nature. Talk about
a two-faced hypocritical pot calling the innocent kettle
black! 'No doubt that spares him from having to *bone up
on how a* manual *can opener works.*'

'Come again?' Rusty asked. Both Harringtons looked totally confused.

'I've decided while Gina's here it'll be more convenient
to eat at my place,' Parish said. 'It'll give us a chance to

discuss the computerization she's doing. Things are so hectic right now, I reckon mealtimes will be the only time I can spare on it.'

'That mean you won't be here for breakfast, either?'

He ate breakfast here, too?

''Fraid so,' he said, unperturbed by the lethal glare Gina sent him.

'Well, I guess that makes sense.' Leanne's expression suggested otherwise. 'You going to make his lunch, too, Gina, or do you want me to still do that?'

Apoplectic with shock, Gina could only manage a strangled gasp.

'You are some piece of work, Parish Dunford!' Gina said as they left the Harringtons'. 'I'm surprised poor Leanne didn't cut up your meal and spoon-feed you! To accuse *me* of taking advantage of that poor woman when you treat her like your own private servant!'

His hand closed on her upper arm and forced her around to look at him. The moonlight made the rigidity in his face more prominent.

'I don't consider Leanne as anything but what she is— the only woman who's earned my unconditional admiration and respect. She's kind, generous to a fault, loyal and trustworthy. And blessedly…' Though his voice rose slightly, his grip on her arm remained constant. 'She doesn't have one pretentious bone in her body! She and Rusty are my oldest and dearest friends. I never have and never will take advantage of either of them.' There was no denying the fierce emotion in his voice, despite the lethally cold way his eyes were narrowed at her. 'Is that clear?'

It came as something of a surprise to realize that she'd genuinely offended this man. Until now she'd thought him as thick-skinned and insensitive as a rhino with rigor mortis.

'Perfectly clear.'

'Good.'

The starry, cloudless sky had let all of the day's remnant heat escape, and a chill westerly breeze had crept onto Malagara under the cover of darkness. Parish knew this. He knew it even as an inner heat rose within him, robbing his body of the ability to feel the cold. Indeed, he felt nothing at all bar an overwhelming need to retract his left arm until Gina Petrocelli's softly curved body was flush against his.

She was as different from the women he was usually attracted to as night was from day. As far removed from his notion of the ideal woman as a ten-year-old hardworking draughthorse was from a million-dollar Thoroughbred yearling. But he wanted to kiss her more than he wanted to take another breath. And they *both* knew it.

'Let go of my arm.' Gina was grateful for the clarity of her voice when her thoughts and emotions were in such turmoil. She was even more grateful when he immediately did as she asked, and downright relieved when he took a step away from her.

'For your information,' Parish said, once again walking towards his house, 'I'd already planned to tell Leanne I'd be changing my eating arrangements.'

She fell into stride with him, head bent, carefully watching each step. 'Was that before or after I admitted I could cook…Parish?'

'Before…*Gina*.'

She looked up to find him smiling. His unnecessary use of her name was an acknowledgment he'd recognized and accepted her subtle overture of friendship in the use of his.

She smiled, too. 'Good.'

'You didn't think I'd be agreeable to the offer of a truce?'

'Huh? Oh, I wasn't saying good to *that*! Although that's good, too,' she added quickly. 'I meant it's good you didn't change your mind about eating at Leanne's just because I can cook.'

'Why's that?'

'Because it means that unlike Leanne, you don't expect me to take over her role and provide you with three meals a day.'

'Right…um, how about two?'

'Parish!'

He laughed. 'Okay, how about one and a light supper at—'

'No way! I'm here to design a computer system for you, not to carry out domestic duties.'

'I'm well aware why you're here. I just didn't think I'd starve because of it.'

He walked with a pseudo-dejected air she didn't buy for one minute. If ever a man came across as being self-reliant it was Parish Dunford.

'You won't starve,' she said dryly. 'Only the good die young.'

'Huh!' He tossed the word over his shoulder. 'So much for a truce!'

'Oh, all right! You win!'

He stopped and turned around. 'I do?'

'Yeah. I'll teach you how to make a sandwich. That way you'll not only be computer literate by the time I leave, but self-sufficient, too!'

'You're all heart.'

Grinning, she walked to him. 'Vulnerability gets me every time.'

'Really?'

'Nope.'

'Didn't think so.'

They walked in a companionable silence for a few strides—or rather, Parish walked and Gina struggled to keep pace with him over the uneven ground. Twice when she would've stumbled, she found herself steadied by his hand on her elbow. Each time the moment she regained her balance he immediately released her. *Which was a good thing*, she told herself.

'You know,' he said, 'I meant what I said about being busy. I have no intention of letting you and this computer stuff disrupt the routine on Malagara.'

'I have no intention of disrupting anything. And I promise you, Parish, this *computer stuff*, as you call it, will streamline the managerial side of this property in ways you've never imagined.'

'Save your breath, Helen's been giving me the spiel for years.'

'Well, obviously she must've sold you on the idea, because I'm here.'

He laughed. 'She didn't so much sell me as wear me down. But as you say, *you are here*. What isn't is a computer.'

'It will be in a couple of days.'

'How do you plan to amuse yourself in the meantime?'

'Acquaint myself with your needs. Your *professional* needs,' she qualified quickly, then blushed because no qualification was necessary. Lord, where was her brain!

'Go on,' he urged, voice dripping with amusement. 'How exactly do you intend to acquaint yourself with my, uh, professional needs?'

'I'd like to examine all the available documentation of your current manual recording procedure. Study your— *damn*!' Once again it was only Parish's lightning quick reflexes that prevented her ending up face down on the rough, dusty ground.

'You right?'

'Fine.'

She didn't sound fine. She sounded dazed and a little breathless.

He was slower releasing her this time. The light, firm pressure of his fingers produced a sensation that, although similar in effect to hitting one's funny bone, was infinitely more pleasant and definitely more sexual! Alarmed, Gina wrenched free of his touch. Parish's expression tensed, and he quickly strode off.

After taking much-needed seconds to calm her pulse and breathing, Gina hurried to catch up with him. 'As I was saying... I want to study accounting procedures, your stock sales and breeding program...'

God, if he walked any faster he'd be at marathon pace!

'And see exactly what sort of program best serves your current set-up. Then I'd like to sit down and discuss your plans for the future so I can design a program that will accommodate them, too.'

She was practically panting by the time she drew level with him. 'It's not worth installing a program that's going to be inadequate for your requirements five years down the track.'

'That sounds like a time-consuming exercise. And I've already explained I don't—'

'*Have a lot of time.* I've got it, all right! Damn! Will you slow down? I'm not a racehorse, for God's sake.'

'Unfortunately you're not a draughthorse, either.'

'Excuse me?'

He shook his head in lieu of explaining his odd remark. 'Didn't you even bring a pair of sneakers?'

'Don't be ridiculous! I couldn't wear sneakers with this! Now where was I?'

'Wanting to waste my time with long—'

'I won't waste anyone's time! If you leave the documentation I need to review, I'll go through it while you're not around. Then if there's anything I need clarification on I'll consult with you at your convenience. Satisfied?'

'You're prepared to accommodate my schedule?'

'Parish, I mightn't know much about cattle stations, but I *am* a professional. I *do* understand schedules!'

'So you're saying you're perfectly willing to work in with whatever suits me?'

'Yes.'

'Anything you need to discuss with me will be fitted into *my* spare time?'

'Yes.'

'Even if that means you'd have to eat when I do?'

'Yes.'

'You're sure about that?'

'*Yes, I'm sure about that*, okay? I'm more than happy to schedule my mealtimes to coincide with yours! I'll even time my questions so you can answer between mouthfuls! Satisfied?'

He laughed. 'Funny, you don't sound happy about it.'

'Trust me, I'm just chock-full of enthusiasm for it. I haven't been this excited since the doctor promised to anaesthetise me before replacing my dislocated shoulder!'

'Watch the step,' he warned. 'How'd you dislocate your shoulder?'

'Doing cartwheels when I found out I needed a root canal.'

'With your sense of humour, mealtimes look like being a regular sideshow.' He held open the screen door and motioned her into the darkened kitchen. 'You will be at breakfast tomorrow, won't you?'

'I'll be there,' she replied, forcing herself to ignore the way her heart skittered as he reached past her, feeling for the light switch. 'Er, what time do you have breakfast?'

The light came on, and she didn't know what was the more blinding, the sudden brightness or his smug, challenging grin.

'Five o'clock, sharp.' His knuckles gently lifted her chin to close her gaping mouth. ''Night, Gina.'

CHAPTER FIVE

'MORNING, Gina. Sleep well?'

'No, I did not. It's so quiet out here it's impossible to get to sleep!' She opened a cupboard, squinted into it then slammed it shut.

'Miss the screech of brakes and the wail of sirens, huh?'

'Yes!' Two more cupboard doors received identical treatment to the first. 'Where the devil do you keep the coffee percolator?'

'Don't have one.'

Parish lip-read well enough to know her response to that hadn't been a blithe *no problem*. 'There's instant coffee in the third cupboard on your right.'

'I *hate* instant coffee.'

'I've made a pot of tea, if you prefer.' She grimaced, grunted and opened the third cupboard on her right.

It was obvious she'd climbed straight out of bed. She wore the robe she'd had on when he picked her up from the airstrip, but in the absence of the extra clothes she'd put on that night to defeat the cold, and with the tie cinched tightly at her waist, Gina Petrocelli didn't come within a bull's roar of *bulky*. Even only half awake she was all slim elegance, subtle curves and shoulder-length, sleep-tousled hair that made Parish itch to comb his fingers through it.

After slumping into the chair across from him, she did it herself, with such sensual laziness Parish almost groaned. For the sake of his sanity he concentrated on his plate of toast and scrambled eggs. 'I take it you're not a morning person.'

'Not when it's not morning.'

'If the sun's up it's morning.'

50

'My point exactly. It's pitch-black outside.'

'It's dawn. Stand out on the veranda, look east and you'll see the prettiest sunrise on earth.'

She squinted at him. 'I can barely sit in this chair and keep my eyes open to see my coffee. Don't taunt me with things that are beyond me.'

Why not? he thought miserably as she stretched an arm to reach the box of cereal and the deep V of her robe widened to display a tantalizing hint of smooth olive skin. *You're doing it to me!*

'I wasn't sure what you liked for breakfast,' he said, seeing her place two wheat bricks on her plate without much enthusiasm. 'I brought those up from the station's main store, in case you were a cereal person, but there's eggs, chops, sausages and steak in the fridge. Help yourself to whatever takes your fancy.'

'This is fine. Thanks.'

She doused the cereal with milk then crushed her spoon into it to break it down. The action drew attention to her elegant long-fingered hand and perfectly manicured nails. Parish found himself thinking that if her hands were even half as soft as they looked, the rest of her skin had to feel like silk. He'd always had a weakness for the cool smoothness of silk.

'Ugh! Sptt!' With barbaric force she spat a mouthful of cereal into the plate. 'It's off!' she said, responding to his no doubt incredulous expression.

'The cereal?'

'The *milk*!'

'Don't be ridiculous. Rusty only brought it up ten minutes ago.'

'I'm telling you the stuff has turned!'

'Milk can't turn in the time it takes to milk the station cow and carry the milk up here.'

'That came from a cow?'

'Course, it came from a cow.'

'You mean it's come *straight* from a cow? From the cow to…to me?'

'Yes.' Parish noted her eyes were definitely wide open now…with horror.

'And you expect me to drink it? When it's…it's *raw*?'

He laughed. 'Not raw—fresh. You're just not used to it being so creamy. Trust me, it'll grow on you.'

'That's what I'm afraid of! Milk is supposed to be pasteurized, homogenized, sterilized and whatever other *ized* they do to make it drinkable! That,' she said, waving a hand at the plastic jug, 'hasn't even been refrigerated!'

'No, it's fresh.' He fired a righteous smile at her. 'It's exactly how God meant milk to be drunk.'

'Wonderful. Then you and God drink it,' she said, rising and marching to the refrigerator. 'But if it's all the same to you, I'll stick with the Louis Pasteur blend that comes in cartons.'

'That'll be difficult. As you can see,' he said, as she searched the shelves of the refrigerator, 'I'm out of cartoned milk. And what with being nearly two hundred kilometres away from the nearest town, it kind of rules out popping down to the shop for some more.'

He shrugged at her despairing expressing. 'You've got a choice. Fresh milk or long life. Course the long-life stuff tastes like crud, but it *does* come in a carton.'

Groaning, Gina put her face in her hands. Never, ever again would she take her local shops for granted! Could her life possibly get any worse?

The sight of a tub of margarine improved her spirits. At least Malagara had progressed beyond churning their own butter, which meant she could have toast.

After eating two slices, washed down with several more cups of coffee, Gina felt she was approaching semi-consciousness. Which, she decided, wasn't necessarily a good thing, because the more alert she became the more conscious she was of the man sitting across the table from her. No man had the right to look so disgustingly healthy and perfectly physically fit when he was clogging his arteries by finishing a second serving of eggs!

'Something wrong?' he asked, becoming aware of her scrutiny.

'No… Um, I've made that list you asked me for…you know, of the things I need to go through.' She fished the piece of paper from the pocket of her robe and pushed it across to him.

'This is pretty long,' he said, when he finally glanced up from it. 'Some of this stuff will have to be brought up from the Downs. I won't be able to get it here for a couple of days.'

'Up from the Downs? Is that some kind of Outback slang?'

Parish's head came up at the note of amusement in her voice. A gently teasing smile played at her mouth, and he couldn't stop himself from responding to its unexpectedness.

'No. The Downs is my grandfather's place, Dunford Downs. It's just outside Rockhampton.' He folded the list and slipped it in his top pocket. 'The rest of what you want to look over should be in the cabinet in my office.'

'You mean the room with the big wooden table and the rickety chair?'

'Yeah. I like the understated look when it comes to furnishings.'

'I noticed.'

'Look, order whatever you think you require to accommodate the computer, but don't go too high tech, okay? We're on single-wire mains electricity, but if the line goes down, we have to revert back to our own diesel plant. If that happens I'd rather not have a whole lot of space-age gadgetry draining the guts out of it.'

'A diesel plant?'

'Our backup power supply. In the wet season, if the main

electricity line gets cut, it can be days or weeks before a repair crew can get through to fix it.'

'You're that isolated out here?'

'Yep. Which is why, when you're through with your coffee, I'll show you how to operate the C.B.' At her quizzical expression he elaborated. 'Rusty and I'll be working out at the strip all day. It's a muster camp out near the old World War Two airstrip, about thirty kilometres southeast of here. I don't expect to be back until after dark, but if you need to contact me urgently you can on the C.B. Up here it's not enough to know how to use a telephone, especially in a medical emergency.'

'You mean like Leanne going into labour.'

'You won't have to worry about that. Rusty's talked her into having a few days of R and R in town.'

'So who's going to look after her kids?'

'The two little ones will go with her. The older ones will stay at the station where they go to school.'

Last night Leanne had explained to Gina how children out here did their lessons by correspondence and the School of the Air, and that usually supervision of lessons fell to the parents. But, she'd told Gina enthusiastically, because a number of the families in the area had grouped together and hired a qualified teacher to supervise the kids, all she was required to do was drive her three eldest kids to the neighbour's each morning and pick them up each afternoon. Gina supposed that compared to being trapped in the house with the high-spirited Harrington children all day, the twice daily eighty-kilometre round trip probably qualified as a luxury! Still, she didn't envy the women who lived out here one single thing.

'I see,' she said. 'So that means that until you and Rusty get back tonight I'll be on my own.'

'Is that a problem?'

'No. I'll have plenty to keep me occupied going through your records.'

Despite her response, she frowned and started nibbling nervously at her lower lip. She looked both sexy and vulnerable at the same time, and something tightened in Parish's chest. He was undecided what he should do—haul her out of her chair and let his own teeth test the softness of her mouth, or say, 'Hey, stuff the job up the strip, I'll stay here with you.' It took considerable effort to ignore the craziness of both impulses.

'Gina, I understand everything up here seems a bit strange—hell, even primitive to you, but there's no need to worry about being alone. For all its isolation, the Malagara homestead is perfectly safe.'

'Oh, I'm not worried,' she assured him airily. 'I was just wondering… Do you think Leanne would mind if I asked her to bring a couple of litres of *real* milk back with her?'

At the sound of the ute's engine, Gina bounded out the screen door into the twilight. It stopped near the other house, and Rusty Harrington's figure climbed from the passenger side a moment before the driver flashed the headlights at her. It might've been meant as a friendly greeting, but Gina had used up all her friendliness.

'About time, Dunford,' she muttered, irritation propelling her feet to the enormous shed that housed the station vehicles, towards which the ute was heading. By the time she got there, Parish was swinging himself from the raised cabin, his boots sending up a puff of dust as they landed on the unsealed ground.

'Gee, Gina,' he drawled, the traces of sweat-smudged dirt on his face not reducing the potency of his grin. 'You didn't have to rush out and welcome me. I'd have come up to the house eventually.'

She ignored the facetious comment. 'Remember telling me snakes up here weren't sociable?'

'They won't bother you if you stay away from them.'

'Believe me, I would if I had a choice, but as we speak there's one in the house!'

'In the house? Well, hell, why didn't you stay put and keep an eye on the damn thing? Damn, it could be any-where by now!'

'I doubt it. It's too drunk to move!'

'Too—' He threw his head back and laughed. 'I take it this particular snake you're referring to is of the six-foot variety and wears size twelve boots.' Her expression was frosty. 'Relax, he's harmless.'

'Sure, now he's passed out on your couch! A few hours ago, when he was guzzling rum and making sexist passes at me, I wasn't so sure. For the first time in my life I was wishing I knew how to use a gun.'

'Aw, Gina, what kind of heartless woman would shoot a friendly old guy like Snake Malone?'

'I didn't say I wanted to shoot *him*. You might have warned me he was coming. He said you knew.'

Parish pulled off his hat and raked his hair. 'Sorry, it slipped my mind.'

'Same as my arrival, huh? Gee, Parish, I'm beginning to suspect the inside of your skull resembles an icerink.'

'Guess that gives us something in common. Your heart being made of ice, and all.'

Gina figured he was probably right, because under the heat of his eyes as they skimmed over her it definitely felt like her insides were starting to melt.

'Just out of curiosity, were you dressed like that when Snake arrived? Cause if so, I wouldn't punish him for any-thing he might've said.' He eased himself back against the ute and hooked his thumbs into his belt. 'Lookin' like you do now, you'd tempt a saint into making a pass, let alone a mere mortal like poor old Snake.'

'Oh, don't be ridiculous!' she snapped, telling herself it was anger, not a blush, burning her face. At the very least it was the oppressive weather, which was what had led her to be dressed as she was in the first place!

The intolerable heat had forced her to forgo style for practicality as she'd tried to find something cool among the winter clothes she'd packed. The best she'd been able to manage was an embroidered waistcoat worn with nothing beneath it and an ankle-length denim skirt that buttoned down the front from waist to hem, although at present it was only buttoned from waist to mid-thigh.

Gina was conditioned to receiving appreciative glances from men, but Parish's inspection of her lower limbs wasn't anywhere fleeting or casual enough to qualify as a glance. She knew she ought to be insulted, or at worst flattered, so it was unsettling to find herself almost giddy under his blatantly masculine appraisal. Though she'd previously thought herself fortunate to be blessed with what she regarded as reasonably good legs, she was revising her opinion in the face of her suddenly weakening knees.

Determined not to budge or show her discomfort, she folded her arms, quickly abandoning the attempt at boredom when she realised the action only pushed her braless breasts higher over the deep V of the waistcoat she wore. Okay, so now she *was* blushing! But as his gaze lifted to her face, she narrowed her eyes, daring him to make one provocative comment!

For long seconds they held each other's gaze. Gina went from being dimly aware of every beat of her pulse and every breath she drew to being alertly conscious of every breath the man facing her took. In turn, the spacious, high-ceilinged building became almost claustrophobic.

What you have here, Gina my girl, her libido whispered, *is a serious case of sexual attraction.*

Great! Just what you need! her brain retorted. *Hormonal anarchy!*

I can handle this, her common sense countered. *Have I ever succumbed to lust overload before? No*!

Just as Gina was telling herself she could rely on her common sense, Parish pushed himself away from the car, and the muscles in her belly did a peculiar little dance she recognized as anticipation. Her heart started thumping so hard against her chest, she half expected the gold buttons on her vest to pop off.

'You know, Gina,' he said, coming to stand only a few feet from her sensation-stunned body, 'I can see we're going to have a lot of disagreements while you're here, but it seems to me our biggest battle is going to be staying out of each other's pants.'

A shocked gasp wedged in her throat, strangling whatever incoherent response she might've uttered.

'Still, I'm willing to give abstinence my best shot,' he told her nobly. 'As long as you do.'

Gina was still trying to figure out what obscene word she should hurl at him first long after he'd taken his conceited, arrogant, perfectly muscled backside out the door.

CHAPTER SIX

OVER the next couple of days, Gina acted as if she'd not heard Parish's remark and he acted as if he'd never made it. The computer and office furniture arrived, and so did her clothes. Unfortunately her sister had interpreted her request for cool, casual clothing as meaning skimpy shorts and jeans.

But vowing nothing would force her into her uncomfortable winter clothes, Gina mentally armed herself with a string of biting comebacks in anticipation of Parish's ridicule about her less than professional style of dress. Strangely none was forthcoming, and Gina found herself feeling something akin to how she imagined a tennis player would at making her first Wimbledon final only to be declared champion simply because her opponent had forfeited! Telling herself she was relieved by his indifference, she threw herself into her work.

While setting up an accounting program was simple enough, given that Parish had only recently purchased the property, she was having a difficult time coming to terms with the magnitude of Malagara's operation. Geographically the property covered approximately thirty-five hundred square kilometres, over thirteen hundred square miles, but she couldn't find a single record of how many head of cattle it carried. Needing this information, she raised the matter one evening while he was having his customary pre-shower beer.

'At this stage I'd only be guessing,' he said, dropping with negligent grace onto the sofa and propping his booted feet on the coffee table, frowning slightly as his spurs further scarred the already battered bit of furniture. 'On a property of this size it's not unusual to carry anywhere between four and five thousand head, but the bloke I bought this from had really let things go. There hasn't been a muster done here for close on two years, so there could be half that number again, or more.

'What I do know,' he went on, setting the beer aside and leaning forward to remove the spurs, 'is there are going to be a lot of cattle who haven't seen a human in a long time, some not at all. This is going to be one hell of a hard muster.'

The smile that emerged on his stubble-shadowed face suggested he relished the thought. It also lent a boyish recklessness to his very earthy, masculine maturity, which Gina found intriguing. He'd be an exciting lover, she mused. Passionate, spontaneous, adventurous and—

Her thoughts screeched to a halt.

Oh, God, the isolation was making her crazy! It had to be, because sane she'd never have been speculating about what kind of lover Parish Dunford would make! Sure, the man was a piece of prime beef, but Gina knew what was good for her when it came to men—something with a lower cholesterol count and a *much* lower testosterone level! And as for spontaneous, adventurous and thrilling sex... Well, naturally she was all for passion in a relationship, but she liked to keep it within the bounds of civilized behaviour and beds.

Heck, she'd stopped using satin sheets after the first time she and her ex-fiancé had slid off them onto the carpet! In hindsight she wondered if that had been an omen, because a few weeks later she'd come to the decision that no matter how she planned to make her matrimonial bed with James, the thought of lying in it for the rest of her life with him was beyond her. Recalling how understanding and accepting James had been when she'd broken off their two-year engagement, it was possible he, too, may have had doubts, but then James was always too polite and urbane to reveal his deepest feelings outside of the bedroom.

That was her problem, she decided. She was suffering sexual withdrawal symptoms. After all, it was over a year since she'd broken up with James, and being celibate for that long after two years of steady, regular, adequate sex—

An alarm bell went off in her head.

Adequate sex? When on earth had she downgraded her relationship with James from satisfactory to adequate, for heaven's sake?

'Gina? What's up?'

If not for the puzzled tone in his voice, Gina would've been certain Parish's intense gaze could read her mind. Irrational as the notion was, she still shook her head to dispel her wayward thoughts. She had to get a grip! Stay focused on matters at hand and stop letting her hormones distract her.

Determined to get on with what she'd been discussing with Parish, she took a controlled breath and lifted her eyes to his. Beneath his dark brows they assessed her with crystal blue interest. He really did have incredible eyes.... What *were* they discussing? Oh, yeah! The stock records...

'Um...'

'Yes?' he prodded.

'You, uh, gave me a list of categories that the cattle are broken up into...' She referred to her notebook. 'Meaters, heifers, breeders, store, et cetera. But I don't understand what they are or where and how I should be dealing with them. I need to know what happens with them so I can decide the best way of collating their records.'

The look on Parish's face and his subsequent sigh implied she was either stupid or wasting his time.

'Look, Parish, you might find my question naive, but I didn't volunteer for this job, and I've no knowledge of the cattle business. I'm working blind here, so if you want a program that's effective you're going to have to *explain* things, not just toss me lists written in terms I know nothing about!'

'Okay, okay,' he said, clearly amused. 'You only had to ask. I think I'll have another beer.' He stood up. 'Can I get you something to drink?'

The offer caught her off guard. 'Huh? Oh! No. No, thanks, I'm fine.'

'Sure?' he asked, from the refrigerator.

She hesitated only for a moment. What the heck! 'Actually, I wouldn't mind a Scotch and water. As long as it's no trouble.'

His laugh carried from the kitchen, and he was still smiling a few minutes later when he returned.

'Coming up with a glass of Bollinger would have caused me some trouble,' he said, handing her the drink. 'Scotch, rum and beer we can always manage out here.'

'Thank you.' Disturbed by his nearness, she quickly moved to sit in the room's only armchair. 'You were going to explain some of the terms you use for cattle,' she prompted, when he continued to simply watch her.

She only breathed again when he resumed his place on the sofa.

'Meaters are bullocks,' he said eventually. 'They're sent straight to the abattoirs. Heifers are female beasts, ones that throw good healthy calves we usually keep because they're good breeders, but others we'll send to the saleyards,' he explained. 'And store cattle are those we plan to ship south to Dunford Downs, where the feed is better, to fatten them up for future sale. Usually they're young steers.'

'What happens to the calves?'

'Once we brand them we usually turn them loose with their mothers and keep them as breeding stock. Some we'll send south to fatten for sale as vealers.'

Gina knew she'd lost focus when she became aware of the mellow feelings the sound of his voice was creating within her. Or was it the hypnotic effect of his unfaltering gaze on her face? How could he be talking about something as mundane as cows and still manage to turn her insides to mush? It was probably just the Scotch on her empty stomach. *Yeah, sure.*

Struggling to give the impression that if she did look half as mesmerized as she felt, it was only due to her previously well-concealed fascination with bovines, she glanced to her notes in the hope of finding another question. 'And what,' she asked, 'is the difference between a bullock and a steer?'

'Age. A castrated beast over three years of age is called a bullock, under three it's a steer.'

'But only if it's castrated?'

'Yep. Otherwise it's a bull calf. Over three and—' one side of his mouth hitched up in amusement '—with all working parts, it's a bull.'

Gina still had a thousand questions, but the distraction of his tall, perfectly honed body rising from the chair caused every one of them to fly from her head. *Lord, but he had a body to die for!*

'Look,' he said, his voice snapping her wayward mind from its admiration of his broad-shouldered, slim-hipped physique. 'I'll have a fair idea of numbers once we finish the muster and do a tally. Until then just concentrate on getting an accounting program up and running.'

'It's practically done,' she told him, dipping her head to hide the heat she felt in her cheeks. 'Basically all that's left to do is to input the figures, and since you've only recently bought the place there's not exactly a lot to do.'

'What about Dunford Downs?'

She frowned. 'What'd you mean, what about Dunford Downs?' A bad feeling settled over her. 'I thought it was only Malagara you wanted computerized.'

'Originally it was…but what can I say?' A slow grin grew on his face. 'You convinced me computerizing Malagara is going to have enormous benefits, so I've decided it makes sense to introduce it to Dunford Downs, too.

Why should only one of my businesses benefit from modernization?'

'But I thought Dunford Downs belonged to your grandfather.'

'It did. I inherited it when he died a couple of years back.'

'Oh… I see.' What she saw was more work. Which meant more time with Parish. She stifled a groan as excitement and dread collided low in her belly. 'So now you want me to design a program to suit *both* properties?'

He nodded. 'Just remember, the Downs and Malagara are two entirely separate operations. I don't want their profits and losses merging.'

'Taxwise that might be the smartest way to set things up, since you own both.'

'An accountant, too, are you?'

'Not certified, no. But my work requires I have a good grasp of taxation matters.'

'Yeah, well, I've got my reasons for wanting to keep the two properties separate. I'm sole owner of Dunford Downs, but I've only got ninety percent of Malagara.'

'Is, er, Dunford Downs as big as this place?'

'Nah! It's only small—about five hundred and twenty square kilometres.'

Small! Yeah, right! 'Look, Parish, what you're asking is going to take an awful lot of time and—'

'No worries. I spoke to Helen, and she said she had no problems with you staying for however long it takes.'

Of course *Helen* wouldn't have a problem with it! *She* had access to unlimited hot water and decent milk! Not to mention airconditioning, a social life and men who didn't threaten a woman with cardiac arrest every time they walked into a room. Actually, considering the devastating smile Parish was flashing now, it was a good thing he favoured living in such a remote and isolated spot. Loose in the city, he'd cause women to riot!

'Don't look so worried, Gina. I've got complete confidence in you being able to get things up and running smoothly.'

'I'm not worried!' *Not about the computer side of things, at least*, she added silently.

'In that case,' he said, 'I'm going to hit the shower. Oh, by the way, traditionally the day before the first muster of the year everyone gets together for a barbecue. The rest of the ringers will be arriving tomorrow morning, and Leanne and the kids will be back. If you haven't made other plans you're welcome to come.'

Other plans? What did he think she was going to do out here in the middle of nowhere? Pop out to the ballet or a gallery opening? She bit back the comment. The invitation had been issued with apparent sincerity. There was no point in being bitchy, especially when she was so heartily sick of her own company.

'Thanks. I…I'd like to.'

'Good,' he said. 'Oh, and I'd really appreciate it if you didn't wear shorts.' His eyes flicked to her legs. 'I can do without starting a muster with a team of ringers with hard-ons.'

She wore jeans. Jeans that, to Parish's eye, looked like they'd been painted on. And damn, what he wouldn't have given to be the bloke holding the paintbrush! All dressed up in her snazzy city clothes, she'd radiated a touch-me-not sexiness that had been more challenging than tempting, but in tight jeans and a barely there knit top, Gina Petrocelli emitted an earthy sensuality that stirred his most primal instincts.

Her hair was caught up in a high, girlish ponytail. Her laugh was light-hearted and utterly unforced as she responded to something Rusty or Snake had just said. Parish would've given his right arm to know what it had been—she never laughed like that at anything he'd said.

At that instant she turned her head. The visual connection between them created an electric current across the fifteen metres of space separating them that froze Parish's lungs in mid breath. Though there was nothing in her demeanour to say so, she felt it, too, he told himself. She had to. Nothing so potent could be one-sided. Or could it? She'd turned away from him with seemingly little effort, while Parish still felt like a lead weight was crushing his chest.

'Idiot!' he muttered, stabbing the barbecue fork into one of the large steaks that sizzled on the grill.

'Who's an idiot?'

Leanne's inquiry jolted his focus to reality. 'Me. For getting stuck with cooking detail. Want to steer everyone over here before I char the lot?'

A few minutes later he was doling out steaks as near to the individual requests of rare, medium and well done as he could manage.

'How do you want it?' he asked, by now barely looking above the height of the plate that was held towards him.

'Medium rare.'

His head came fully up at the sound of Gina's voice.

'And half the size of what you're about to drop on my plate,' she added.

'Not hungry, or is it you don't trust my cooking?'

'Actually I am hungry,' she told him. 'And as for your cooking…well, I'll try anything once.'

'Now there's a leading statement.'

'Following it would be unhealthy.'

Laughing, he reached for a knife and cut a thick, juicy steak in half.

'My God,' she said, pulling her plate back before he could deposit the meat on it. 'I said medium rare. That's raw!'

'What? That steak is so close to perfect it amazes even me.'

She gave him a droll look. 'Parish, that steak is so close to its natural state it'll moo if I put a fork into it.'

'Picky, picky,' he muttered, selecting another piece of meat and cutting it in half. 'How's this?'

'Fine.' She smiled at him as he put it on her plate. 'Thanks. Guess this means I win, huh?'

'Win what?'

'The hold-out on who'd cook for whom first.'

Parish didn't pretend not to understand what she was talking about. 'The logical thing *would* have been to have struck a deal over the cooking,' he agreed.

'True. Guess this means I owe you a dinner.'

'If it bothers you I won't hold you to it.'

'No!' She gave a tiny shrug. 'I mean, fair is fair. Besides, I enjoy cooking for someone other than myself.'

'Hey, Parish!' the man behind Gina interrupted. 'What's the hold-up? I've been standin' here so long me belly thinks me throat's been cut.'

Gina immediately uttered an apology and stepped aside.

'Keep your shirt on, Blue. I'm not about to let you starve when I need you ready to muster tomorrow.' Selecting the piece of meat the stockman pointed to, Parish dropped it onto the plate.

There were only a handful of people waiting for steaks. Nearly everyone was already sitting down eating, yet Gina had made no move to join them. With another woman, he'd have said she was waiting for him so they could sit together. With Gina he couldn't be sure.

'Help yourself to some salad and veggies,' he said, motioning towards the table to the left of the barbecue. 'Leanne's famous for her potato salad, so you'd best get in while there's still some left.'

'Um, would you like me to get some for you? I mean...if you're serving everyone else it might be gone before you get some.'

The hesitant offer was enough to have him reaching for

a plate. 'Thanks,' he said, placing it in her outstretched hand.

'Anything special you'd like?'

His eyes held hers. 'Yeah, there is…but I'll let you decide what I get.'

Her thick lashes were lowered before Parish could distinguish if it was alarm or desire that flared in her eyes. If his own feelings were any gauge, it was both. There was something scary about craving something you knew would be bad for you, but caring less about the danger than the thought of not getting it.

Gina had to take everyone's word for it that Leanne made the best potato salad this side of the Black Stump, because with the weight and warmth of Parish's denim-covered leg pressed against her own at the cramped table, her hormones had short-circuited her tastebuds. With him this close she could have been eating live snake and not known it!

The way his breath brushed her neck or shoulder as he used whispered asides to explain some comment or expression the assembled ringers made, which was totally incomprehensible to a city person, sent tiny sparks of electricity skittering through her blood and left her more bemused than anything any of the stockmen had said.

She could only assume that her wanton reaction to Parish didn't manifest itself externally, since no one had thrown a bucket of water over her, but desperate to give her nerves some respite from his nearness, she leapt at the chance to help Leanne dish up desert. Once that was done she didn't return to her place beside him, but took a chair between two of the stockmen at the other end of the table, then spent the rest of the evening subtly avoiding being within a four-metre radius of him.

And he knew it, damn him!

She *knew* he knew. It was evident in the initial puzzled frown he gave her when she excused herself from the group of people she was chatting with within seconds of his arrival, and in the way he'd then deliberately followed her from one group to another, with wicked amusement lighting up his too blue eyes. Wherever she moved he was either right on her heels or watching her with an expression that told her he was thoroughly enjoying their game and challenging her to try to make it harder. Except Gina wasn't interested in playing! In the end she'd pleaded tiredness and quietly slipped away from the gathering.

Now, though, he had her cornered.

Squeezing her eyes shut, she told herself to ignore the knock on her bedroom door. He might be good-looking, but not even *he* could look through solid timber.

A second knock came.

Ignore it, Gina. If you really were asleep you wouldn't hear it.

The contact of knuckles on wood was marginally louder the third time. How could a sound produce guilt? Especially when there was nothing to be guilty about? It wasn't a crime not to answer a door.

A fourth knock. 'Gina...you awake?'

The question was asked in a low, husky tone that seemed to reach into the room and caress her skin. Her heart raced, pumping blood and adrenaline through her at light speed. She didn't like him, she told herself. Her physical reactions were irrational. But her body wasn't listening to her brain, and she clutched the sheets, fearing that if she didn't occupy her hands, her arms might stretch across the room and open the door of their own accord. If she didn't answer he'd think she was asleep. Not responding to a question wasn't lying, it was—it was *ignoring*, she reasoned. Ignoring someone might be rude, but...well, sometimes rudeness was necessary for self-preservation.

This was one of those times. Because the truth was she didn't trust herself not to throw herself into his arms the minute that door was no longer between them. The truth scared the hell out of her.

She wasn't aware she'd been holding her breath until it came out in a rush once Parish's footsteps had disappeared down the hall. There was an immediate relaxing of the muscles in her jaw, and her fingers uncurled. It took considerably longer for her heart rate to slow. Trying to overlook the slight sense of regret that niggled at her, she reassured herself that she'd done the right thing. To have given in to Parish's attempt to speak with her would've been on par with putting a six-week-old bunny in a cage with a starving greyhound. Her analogy brought its own questions. Clearly she perceived herself as the helpless rabbit, but was it Parish or her own suddenly ravenous libido that represented the dog?

Sighing at the inanity of her thoughts, Gina rolled on her side and determinedly closed her eyes. All she needed was a good night's sleep. By morning she'd be mentally and emotionally fortified enough to face Parish over breakfast.

What limited comfort that assertion provided, however, vanished when she woke to find Parish already gone. Disappointment warred with anger over the fact that he hadn't bothered to say goodbye.

But then that's your *fault, isn't it?* her conscience taunted.

CHAPTER SEVEN

'HEY, Parish, I'm gonna call Leanne on the two-way and check in. Any message for Gina?'

Yeah, stay the hell out of my head! Parish thought, though he muttered a negative response to Rusty's question. No point advertising the fact his mind had been on something other than what it should have for most of the day. Mustering was hard, dangerous work, and the men he'd hired were all well-respected, experienced ringers. As boss he wouldn't win any brownie points from them for giving the job only a smidgen of the attention it deserved.

Rusty's departure acted like a signal for the other men who, with murmured references to the long, hard day facing them tomorrow, began getting to their feet and exchanging good-nights. Parish remained on the log he was sitting on and stared into the flickering flame of the camp fire, which was more tradition than necessity since their recently finished meal had been prepared on a state-of-the-art butane gas cooker. In a few hours he was due to relieve Blue, who'd drawn first shift at keeping an eye on the cattle they'd mustered and yarded today, and Parish knew he should be catching a couple of hours of sleep while he could. Of course, knowing he should sleep and being able to were two entirely different things.

Usually the first day of mustering after The Wet left him feeling bone weary but energized and eager to start the second. Tonight the only thing he could think about was getting the next six days out of the way quickly, so he could get back to the homestead and see Gina. And *that* had him worried. The only other time he'd looked forward to a mus-

ter ending before it'd barely started he'd been nineteen and
trying to ride with a fractured collarbone.

'Which only goes to prove she's a real pain in the neck,'
he complained dryly. Unfortunately the problem was that
whenever an image of her popped into his head, he felt the
discomfort in a somewhat lower section of his anatomy!
Sighing, he stood and tossed the dregs of his tea into the
fire, but even the immediate hiss of liquid hitting flame was
reminiscent of the relationship between Gina and himself.

If they weren't total opposites, then they came damn
close. Nothing he'd observed about Gina Petrocelli in the
time he'd known her had struck him as being genuinely
impulsive. Everything about her was civilized, modernized,
polished and socially correct. Even her temper was within
the realms of acceptability. Sure, she'd flipped out because
her travel arrangements had been screwed up. And she'd
been irritated by the concept of having to adapt her bathing
routine to the vagaries of an antiquated hot water service.
But Parish wondered if she'd ever once been white-hot,
spitting mad about anything but a small lapse of social nice-
ties. She reminded him of his mother, a Brisbane socialite
who became almost rabid at the thought of caterers using
the wrong china pattern but was untouched by the day-to-
day problems facing people on the land.

Like his mother, Gina Petrocelli came across as being
affected only by things that threatened the normality of *her*
existence. And still he was attracted to her. Fascinated by
her quick, sharp wit and mesmerized by her Italian beauty,
he wanted her more than he could remember wanting any
woman. Wanted her with a passion he could almost taste.
Not for the long haul, but for a quick, no-strings liaison
from which he suspected they'd both derive enormous
physical pleasure.

Not needing the disturbing sensations such thoughts triggered, he crawled into his sleeping bag telling himself he
was so bone tired, he wouldn't have had the strength to

make a move on her if she'd miraculously appeared on the spot, naked, and burrowed in beside him. A dry laugh broke from his throat. *Right!*

'What's so funny, boss?' Blue asked from a few metres away.

'I'm practising reverse psychology on myself.'

'Yeah?' came the bemused response. 'Is it workin'?'

'The idea is to stop it from working.'

'Oh, I see... I think.'

By late Tuesday afternoon Gina was nearly insane from the silence. No, not silence—*loneliness*. She liked solitude, but only up to a point, a point she'd passed around three o'clock in the morning when she'd still been lying awake, staring at the ceiling and mentally rehashing past conversations she'd had with Parish Dunford, then going on to visualizing new ones. Ones that invariably ended with him kissing her! Deciding she really had to get out more or crack up completely, she gratefully accepted Leanne's invitation to dinner, easing her guilt about creating extra work for the poor woman by insisting she'd provide dessert.

While apple pie wasn't exactly what Gina considered a culinary challenge, she'd made it because Leanne had said, 'Sure! But try and keep it simple because the kids tend to get hyperactive on chocolate and rich stuff.'

Though Gina found the thought of the Harrington kids on sugar-overload downright scary, they were, however, thrilled to see her when she arrived at their home that evening. She could tell from their welcoming shouts of, 'Great, you're here! Now maybe we can finally eat!'

'Am I late?' she asked Leanne, surprised to see Snake was also there, since she'd assumed that, with the exception of thirteen-month-old Billy, the entire male population of Malagara were out playing cowboys.

'Relax, you're not late. They're just naturally rude. Besides, I made the mistake of mentioning you were bringing apple pie, so they're anxious to get the vegetables out of the way.'

Sharing a table with the chattering, excitable four Ks, as Gina had come to think of the girls, a food-flinging toddler and Snake, who'd mastered the art of swallowing without chewing, was a unique experience for Gina. And although she obligingly answered the stream of inquisitive, bordering-on-rude questions the girls fired at her and couldn't help laughing at the risqué joke the oldest K delivered even as Leanne fought to maintain a disapproving face, she felt more comfortable once the children had scoffed down their apple pie and deserted the table.

'So how come you're not out mustering with the rest of them?' she asked Snake as Leanne returned from taking an armload of empty plates to the kitchen with an oversized teapot.

''Cause I'm a mechanic, not a ringer,' the man replied. 'Not everyone's fool enough to go careering through scrub after wild cattle on horseback.'

'Snake's the station mechanic on the Downs,' Leanne explained as she filled Gina's cup. 'He's just helping out up here until Parish finds someone to do the job permanently.'

'Oh.' Though born and raised on Italian coffee, Gina studied the contents of her cup with something akin to dread. The tea was so thickly black, she imagined a spoon could stand upright in it unaided, at least until it dissolved completely. And if the smell was anything to go by, the steaming liquid was probably as tarlike in taste as appearance. It was only the recollection of what milk tasted like out here that stopped her from asking for some.

'Do all cattle stations have full-time mechanics?' she inquired, in an effort to put off taking a sip of the stuff for a tad longer.

'The big ones do.' It was Snake who replied. 'Can't run the risk of a bore breakin' down an' cattle bein' left without water. Then there's the homestead pumps, generator an' station vehicles… Plenty to keep a bugger busy,' he assured her.

'I see. So who's taking care of things at Dunford Downs if you're here?'

'The 'prentice I got down there'll have his ticket in a few months. I figured he could hold the fort on his own a while,' Snake said with gruff confidence, then added, 'station manager'll lemme know if he can't.'

Gina nodded, then bravely took a sip of her tea, swallowed and reached for the sugar bowl. Good God! Snake could probably use the stuff cold to clean engines!

The ensuing half hour of conversation with Leanne and Snake was most enlightening. For example, she learned that Dunford Downs was considered a showcase among cattle properties and that it had a permanent staff of eight, which included a housekeeper, the new station manager and his wife, three full-time ringers—additional ones were hired on a short-term basis from time to time—the apprentice mechanic and Snake. She also discovered that when the muster was over, Parish would start looking for permanent employees for Malagara. Currently everyone was on short-term contracts.

'What about you and Rusty?' she asked Leanne. 'Will you stay on?'

'Don't have much choice,' Leanne said, smiling. 'Right now Rusty is so excited about Parish's plans for Malagara I doubt he'd be shifted with dynamite. Still, we've never stayed put in one place more'n a few seasons, so beyond that it's anyone's guess.'

Gina immediately felt sorry for the woman, forced to move her family from one place to another solely on the whim of a man, but more so for her children, who were denied the stability of growing up in a constant community. She knew only too well how difficult that could be. But at least the Harrington kids had their mother available virtually twenty-four hours day, and a father who, when not mustering, came home for dinner each night.

It wasn't long before the children loudly reappeared, Billy crying and two of the Ks offering a did not, did too routine by way of explanation. Snake, showing classic male sensitivity, immediately got to his feet, thanked Leanne for dinner and announced he was 'headin' home to bed and some peace an' quiet!' Personally Gina was ready to head home and pump the corrosive tea from her stomach, but unlike Snake she couldn't in good conscience go off and leave her fatigued hostess with the dishes.

When Leanne went to organize the three youngest children for bed, Gina tried to cajole the two older girls, who were bickering over what television show they were going to watch, into helping her with the washing and drying up. But in a show of unity any trade union would've been proud of, both conveniently remembered unfinished homework.

'Sorry, but Mum always says homework comes first,' the younger of the two said virtuously.

'Yeah,' her sister added. 'A good education is the platform to the future.'

Yeah, right. Don't trip on your haloes, girls! she thought as the two scampered from the room.

While she was the last person to advocate kids being forced to take on their parents' responsibilities or female children being groomed solely for domesticity, she considered the Harrington girls particularly insensitive to just how hard their mother's life was, because despite her assurances to the contrary, Leanne looked totally exhausted. Gina recognized the look only too well. She'd seen it on her mother's face for most of the first fourteen years of her life.

With a sigh, she plunged her hands into the sudsy water in the sink, thinking longingly of the dishwasher in her kitchen at home.

A short time later the sudden intrusion of a crackly male

voice startled her almost as much as the excited Leanne, who came tearing from the other part of the house.

'I'll get it! I'll get it!' she announced, hurrying towards the small table in the corner of the room that was home to the C.B. radio. Snatching up the handset, she burst into a greeting sprinkled with endearments, and it didn't take a genius to work out the caller was Rusty. Wishing to offer the woman some privacy, despite the fact nothing in the loudness of Leanne's voice suggested she wanted it, Gina turned to resume the task of washing the dishes.

She knew she'd failed to make herself entirely oblivious to the conversation when she found herself instantly on alert at the mention of Parish's name. Becoming completely still, she unashamedly strained to hear what was being said, and though Leanne's nearness made her words unmistakable, slight static meant Rusty's were less clear.

'If yer ask me he's royally ticked 'bout somethin',' Rusty complained. 'He's workin' like there's no tomorrow and the whole thing needed to be finished yest'dee!'

Leanne laughed. 'Havin' trouble keeping up with him, are you, honey?'

'Even his horse is havin' trouble keepin' pace with him!'

Immediately Rusty's voice receded as the image of Parish astride a horse with his hat pulled low over his eyes flashed into Gina's head. Her mind portrayed the mental picture as an incredibly sexy one, where his rock-hard muscles and chest glistened in the sun with baby-oil sleekness.

'Idiot!' she muttered, nearly smashing a dish as she chinked it against the tap. It was a muster, not a fashion-magazine shoot, for God's sake! The guy wasn't likely to be riding around without a shirt! Besides, if he was glistening with anything it would be sweat, not oil! She loathed sweaty men!

'Gina!'

She jumped at the sound of her name, and feeling a fool spun around to Leanne. 'What?'

'Do you want to talk to Parish?'

'To Parish?'

'Yeah.'

'Why?'

Leanne shrugged, eyeing her strangely. 'I dunno…about the work you're doing or whatever.'

'Oh. Um, er…' Gina's mind went as blank as a virgin hard drive, but her pulse rate was wanton. 'Does he want to speak with me?' She found herself holding her breath as Leanne put the question to Rusty.

'Rusty says no, but he can go get him if you want him for anything.'

She shook her head. Why should she want him when he didn't want to talk to her? Besides, he'd be back in five days. Any questions she had could wait until then. Five days wasn't very long. Five days was nothing at all. A lousy hundred and twenty hours. She had plenty to keep her busy, heaps of things to do that didn't need discussing with him. The very last person she needed for anything was Parish Dunford!

Both the heat and dust were so thick, Parish felt like he had to chew and swallow before he could speak.

''Hoy! Farrelly!' he roared to the young ringer working on the second of the bronco horses. 'Take a break. The boys in the branding yard need a breather.' In truth, Farrelly's less than accurate roping meant that for every bull the bloke dragged up the branding ramp, Parish did two. Calling a break would give him the opportunity to reassign the kid to another task when they resumed without hurting his feelings. The young bloke was eager enough, but Parish didn't have the time to let him perfect his roping skills on the job, and he could tell from the expression on Rusty's face as he approached that he, too, had noticed the problem.

'Want Blue to take over from him?'

'Yep. Otherwise we'll never get finished.'

'I wouldn't say that,' Rusty said dryly. 'Not with you workin' at breakneck speed. What's the rush? We goin' for a Guinness book record or somethin'?'

Parish stared at his friend. 'I allowed seven days for this first muster,' he said. 'We're a day late starting the branding as it is. I don't want to get any further behind.'

Rusty raised an eyebrow. '*Seven* days. Well, that's good news! The way you've been working yerself the last two an' a half I figured we only had three days to get it done.' A suggestive smile played on his mouth. 'Person might think yer were in a hurry to get home.'

'Then they'd be wrong.'

Rusty threw his head back and laughed. 'Bull!'

Tugging his hat lower, Parish turned his horse away before he made an even bigger liar out of himself.

Wednesday night she ate dinner alone. Or rather she sat at the kitchen table and moved her meal around her plate without an audience. Every few minutes she'd catch herself staring longingly at the silent C.B. and tell herself she needed therapy.

'How is it I've regressed into teenage crush syndrome when only a couple of weeks ago I was a thinking intelligent woman?' She swore. '*And why the hell am I sitting here talking to myself?*'

The answer to both questions was multiple choice— Parish Dunford. Parish sexy-as-hell Dunford. Parish rough-edged Dunford. Parish the-last-man-she-should-be-attracted-to Dunford. And, of course, all of the above.

'Damn! Damn! Damn!' She thumped the table. 'And damn!'

Leaping to her feet, she snatched up the plate containing her mutilated meal and stomped to the sink. She was angry for no logical reason and edgy as hell because of it, and the isolated soundlessness of Malagara didn't help, either.

What she longed for was the luxury of her state-of-the-art CD player and a stack of the loudest rock records she possessed. Unfortunately those things were sitting in her perfectly appointed, airconditioned penthouse in Sydney, and the ancient radio Parish kept in the living room only had an AM band, which to her horror she'd learned yesterday, was jammed on a country and western station. If there was a plus to be found in her current situation it could only be she'd not yet sunk to the level where line dancing looked like a solution for her problems.

Dishes rinsed, she momentarily considered putting in a few more hours on the computer, then immediately dismissed the idea. She'd made one mistake after another today. There was no sense in compounding them. A walk in the fresh air would probably do her some good, but if she did that she wouldn't hear the C.B. if—

'Gina!' she roared. 'He's not going to call. If he hasn't had reason to call in three days, he's not going to call tonight!'

She opened the cupboard and snared the half bottle of Scotch and the first glass at hand. The latter's shape and the remnants of a yellow label stuck to it proclaimed its previous life as a Vegemite jar. Typical. Crystal would never cut it on Malagara!

Gina poured herself an inch or so of the liquor before putting the bottle back on the shelf. Picking up the glass, she headed for her room, pausing only for an instant to glare at the C.B.

'I'm going to bed,' she told it. 'And damn you, Parish Dunford.' She jiggled the glass. 'You aren't going to keep me awake tonight!'

Parish couldn't sleep. He'd been lying here, staring skyward, in this miserable sleeping bag for nearly two hours. It didn't help that the thousands of stars twinkling overhead reminded him of the glitter that came into *her* eyes every time she bested him. Nor did the knowledge that right at this moment she was probably sound asleep, her delectable little body curled up in a warm, comfortable bed, when it was her fault he was ready for life membership in Insomniacs Anonymous.

It was, he decided, time for him to take some affirmative action based on the *eye-for-an-eye theory*.

Gina would've liked to blame what was occurring on a dream, except she wasn't asleep. Which meant she was going insane. There was no history of mental instability in her family, albeit she didn't know much about her ancestors on her natural father's side, but even so, she seriously doubted her desertion from the ranks of what was generally regarded as normal was the result of her genetic makeup. No, it was a pretty safe bet that the decline in her mental stability was sleep deprivation.

Sleep deprivation and Parish Dunford.

Even now, lying wide awake and alone in the darkness, she could hear him calling her as clearly as if he was in the next room. Calling her over and over in a crackly voice that for some reason made her think of Rusty. God knew why, Rusty wasn't—

'Oh, my God!' she gasped as her feet hit the floor running. He was on the C.B.! He was calling her on the radio! She fairly sprinted down the hall, skidding to a barefooted halt at the end to turn left into the living room.

CHAPTER EIGHT

'GINA! Gina...Gina, this is Parish. Answer, dammit!'

'I will! All right!' she responded tersely. 'Just gimme a second!' Gazing at the array of switches and dials, she tried to recall how he'd shown her to use the machine. Call her conservative, but give her a cellular phone any day!

'Hello... Hello, can you hear me?' She depressed and released the button on the handset a couple of times as she spoke.

'Gi...hear...are you...' Parish's voice came and went between dead patches and static.

Mumbling with frustration, she jiggled the button some more and spoke again. 'Parish, I can't understand what you're saying. Is something wrong?'

'Gina...stop push...button...can't...no ne...you...'

What was he talking about? She wasn't pushing—

Catching sight of her hand, she guiltily lifted her thumb from the button on the side of the handset. Instantly Parish's conversation began flowing evenly into the room.

'Listen. Hold it down when you're speaking and release it when I am. Do you understand? You only hold it down when you're speaking.'

To be actually hearing his voice again was enough to make her forgive the dealing-with-a-two-year-old-tone that he used, but he didn't have to know that!

Grinning, she brought the handset to her mouth, and with her thumb steady on the transmit button replied.

'Did you get me up in the middle of the night just to patronize me or is there another reason for this call?' She lifted her thumb and heard him chuckle. The sound created a warmth deep inside her.

'Yeah, there is. I wanted to be sure if there was an emergency you'd know how to answer the C.B.'

'Well, then, mission accomplished,' she responded. 'Does that mean I get to go back to bed now?'

'It wasn't exactly a smooth execution.' There was amusement in his voice.

'It wasn't exactly an emergency.'

'You didn't know that.'

'I do now.'

'I think you need practice using the C.B. so you feel more comfortable with it. You can get that by bringing me up to date with how the computer stuff is coming along.'

'Fine. The program's not giving me any problems.' *He* was causing her more problems than any program ever would.

'Good. Er, so how are things in general?'

Smiling, she eased back in the chair. He wanted to talk with her. No, *chat* with her. For no readily apparent reason, he'd called her at—she glanced at her watch—ten-forty at night. The notion filled her with feminine satisfaction. Smirking like the proverbial Cheshire, she moved her thumb to the transmit button.

'Things aren't any different than before you left,' she said coolly. 'What were you expecting to happen, Parish? That Leanne and I would start throwing wild parties and entertaining men?'

Gritting his teeth, Parish slumped against the passenger seat in the four-by-four. Though there'd been a distinctly teasing tone in her question, the thought of Gina with any man but himself didn't thrill him. He wanted reassurance that her mind was as obsessively occupied with thoughts of him as his was with her.

'Wild parties and men?' he said. 'Not a chance! I know Leanne too well to think that.'

'But you don't know me. Fair enough,' she told him. 'Let me reassure you by saying I've been the model house guest in your absence. I'm still getting up at the crack of dawn even though there's no one here to make me. And I've restrained the inherent decadence that urges me to take two showers in the same day. Does that satisfy you?'

He chuckled. 'Not by a long shot, Gina. Not by a very long shot! But you know, I didn't say you couldn't have two showers, only that you couldn't have two hot ones... Unless of course you wanted to share one. Had you taken up that option, well, then, you wouldn't need to ask about what satisfies me.'

The seductive quality of his voice sent shivers down her spine. Not trusting what might come out of her mouth, she released her thumb and drew a long, steadying breath. As she did Parish spoke.

'You know, Gina, if I had the choice of a hot or cold shower right now, I'd have to take cold.'

The conversation wasn't conducive to going back to bed and falling asleep, but Gina didn't care. There was something deliciously exciting yet safe about talking with him like this, and for the first time in her life she felt the urge to flirt.

'Gee, Parish.' She practically purred his name. 'Why's that?'

'Take a guess,' he challenged.

'Um...because you're really tired but you want to stay awake?'

'Believe me, Ms Petrocelli, staying awake hasn't been a problem for me these last few nights. Which is probably hard for someone who sleeps as soundly as you do to understand.'

'Don't make assumptions about things you know nothing about, *Mr. Dunford*. I'm usually a very light sleeper.' *Especially since I met you,* she added silently.

'If you're such a light sleeper, how come you didn't hear me knocking on your door the other night?'

'It just so happens I was extremely tired Sunday night.'

'How did you know it was Sunday night I knocked, Gina?' he asked, and she could have kicked herself.

'Lucky guess.'

'Liar.' He made the word sound like an endearment. 'I wonder what would've happened if I'd followed my instincts and just walked in.'

'I'd have followed my instincts and thrown something at you,' she retorted quickly.

'Ah, but you wouldn't have known... Remember, you were supposedly asleep in bed.'

'Even in bed my instincts and reflexes are good.' She felt herself blush. Oh, God! Had she really *said* that? Parish's laughter told her she had.

'I guess I'll have to take your word on that...for now. I should warn you, though, Gina, on a C.B. you ought to be careful of what you say. Anyone could be listening in, and they might misconstrue an utterly innocent conversation like this.'

Gina knew she should be shocked by his revelation, and she was—a little. But while she might've been ignorant of the fact that they could've been eavesdropped on, the knowledge that Parish hadn't been and was still prepared to openly flirt with her seemed almost honourable. She smiled. It might've been a bizarre conclusion to draw, but she couldn't help feeling happy anyway.

'Does your lack of response mean you're angry at me?' His voice sounded concerned at the possibility.

'No, Parish, I'm not angry.'

'Good.'

The wealth of sincerity in his one-word reply sent heat coiling around her heart, and for long moments she was content to just sit there and focus on the sensation. She wondered if the silence of the radio meant Parish was perhaps doing the same thing.

'Parish,' she said. 'I've heard all about silence being

golden and all, but I think it's time you let me and whoever else is out there in listener land go to bed.'

Again she was surrounded by the warmth of his laughter. 'Okay, I guess you're right. Some of us ought to be allowed to get some sleep.'

'Good night, Parish,' she said, hearing her reluctance to end the conversation in the words.

'Good night, Gina…sleep well. I doubt I will, but I'll call you tomorrow and let you know. That okay with you?'

She nodded before it dawned on her he couldn't see her. 'I…I'd like that,' she said softly into the handset.

'Me, too…'

The radio went dead, but Gina felt positively reborn.

Sleep came easily to her that night, as it did the next and the next, when, after bidding Parish good-night on the C.B., she climbed into bed. If anyone did bother to listen in on or accidentally stumbled onto their nightly conversations, Gina imagined they'd find them trite and inane, but for her they were much more.

Strangely, communicating with Parish using only the senses of hearing and speech without the distractions of physical appearance and social differences heightened her awareness of him. The nightly exchanges left her smiling with a feeling of wholesome wellbeing and yet sensually charged. The latter was as confusing as it was exciting, for while she could comprehend and accept that she was sexually attracted to Parish Dunford, she was disconcerted by the primitive, raw earthiness of the attraction.

In the past, her experiences with sex had been confined to the bounds of a long-term engagement with a nice, sensible man who wanted the same things from life she did—in effect, sex with an emotional safety net. By comparison, she'd always regarded the hot, torrid relationships depicted in films and novels in the same light as parachute jumping—daring, exciting, but not something she ever wanted to engage in personally.

An affair with Parish Dunford would be like skydiving without a chute.

'Either you've taken to smokin' something stronger than tobacco or you're sufferin' delayed shock or somethin'.'

Parish looked up from his lunch into the face of the man who stood towering over him. 'Rusty, I don't have a clue what you're rabbiting on about.'

'I'm talkin' about it being the morning made in hell an' you grinnin' like a fifteen-year-old who just got his first lay!'

'You know, Rusty, with a little finetuning you could be a psychic.'

'As opposed to you, who's a psycho?'

Fighting down a grin, Parish moved over to let the other man share the short log he sat on. 'Relax, mate, it's not like we haven't had cattle bust out of a holding yard before. I'll take one of the fellas with me after lunch and go after the escapees. It's an inconvenience, but no real drama.'

'Only days ago you were worryin' about fallin' behind, now you're actin' like Polly-bloody-Anna.' Rusty studied him intently. 'Forget what I said about you sufferin' from shock, it's gotta be either drugs or love.'

'I don't do either, you know that, Rusty.'

'There's a first time fer everythin', they tell me.'

'Don't believe everything you hear.' Parish stood up and stretched his arms above his head. 'Well, mate, I've got some mongrel bullocks to muster.' Scooping up his saddle, he headed towards where the fresh horses were tethered.

'Take care,' Rusty said. 'Doesn't pay to get too cocky.'

The advice made Parish turn back to stare at his friend. 'Hey, when was the last time I got careless mustering?'

The other man gave a wry smile. 'Fer the sake of my health, I won't answer that question. But who says I was warnin' you 'bout your attitude to bullocks?' he asked casually. 'Everyone knows most horn injuries are caused by *cows*. Reckon that proves a bloke oughtn't forget just how unpredictable the female of *any* species can be.' He laughed at the two-finger gesture Parish used as a response.

'Did I wake you?'

'No. I was just doing a dummy balance of the Dunford Downs accounts to test an idea I had.' *While I sweated on you calling*, Gina added silently.

'Did it pan out?'

'Not as well as I'd hoped, but I'm confident I can iron out the kinks. Um, how was your day?' Now there was a scintillating question.

'Long, hot and tiring. I've only just finished yarding some stubborn runaways who thought they'd get the better of us.'

'But it's almost midnight. How can you round up cattle in the dark?'

'You've been watching too many Yank horse operas, Gina. We Aussies muster cattle, we don't round 'em up.' The amusement in his tone stopped the remark from being a genuine criticism.

'At any rate, we weren't mustering in the dark, we were yarding. I'll take you out to one of the camps one day and you can see how it's done. Watching a muster is really the only way for a city slicker to comprehend what's involved.'

The invitation to the camp was probably only a throw-away line, so Gina remained silently noncommittal on the subject. 'Where are you now? Still at, um, Tea Party, is it?'

'Nope. Left there this morning. We're at the strip camp now. Which is why we were yarding late. Tomorrow we start all over again mustering the cattle in this area.'

It surprised her how easily she recognized the tiredness in his voice when previously she'd only noted the distinctions between confidence, humour and sarcasm. That she now could identify the more subtle nuances of his tone was disturbing enough for her to want to ignore it.

'With an ounce of luck,' he continued, 'we'll have the branding done by Saturday and head back to the bullock paddock Sunday.'

Her heart flipped, because she knew that once the cattle were in the bullock paddock, the men would be returning to the homestead. 'So, um, you'll be back Sunday night?' she asked.

'If I get my way. If not, count on seeing me Monday.'

Panicked at just how much she *was* counting on it, and how much of him she wanted to see, Gina tried to steer the conversation in other directions.

'By the way, Parish, are you personally responsible for dreaming up fanciful names like Tea Party and the strip for the muster sites? Or did you get ripped off by an advertising agency?' she asked.

He laughed. 'I'll plead guilty to Tea Party, but not the rest. They were the camp names when I bought the place. Take a look at the maps on the wall above you.'

The maps in question were tacked to a cork noticeboard, which hung on a sloppy angle above the radio set-up. There were two of them, an aerial photograph, presumably of Malagara, with black ink crosses marked in various places, and a standard map without the hindrance of tree foliage, giving a clearer image of the rivers and roads that streaked the property.

'I see them,' she said, since he was obviously waiting for some kind of response.

'Okay. The crosses represent the muster camps. The one called the strip on the southwest boundary is close to an old World War Two airstrip, hence the name. In the southern corner is Long Way Camp, named Long Way because…it's a long way there and a long way back.'

She rolled her eyes and depressed the transmit button on her handset. 'I'm so staggered by the amount of thought that went into that one, I can't wait to hear what the rest of them are called.'

'The one right in the far eastern corner, in the elbow of the two boundary fences, is called the Elbow. You with me on that, Gina? Tell me if it gets confusing.'

'Very funny! But that doesn't explain *Tea Party*.'

'Ah, yes! Well, Tea Party was originally called the Number One, because traditionally it was the first area mustered. But not long after we got here, young Karlee went missing, and we couldn't find her. Four hours into the search, Ron Galbraith spotted her from his plane out at Number One and radioed her location. I was the closest to her, and when I found her, the little wretch was sitting in a circle with two dolls and a plastic tea set.' He laughed. 'She told me she wanted to have a tea party without her older sisters messing it up!'

Even though Gina laughed, she realized that out here the happy ending could just as easily have been the opposite. The history of people getting lost and dying in the Australian Outback stretched from the beginning of Anglo settlement, over two hundred years ago, to the modern day. In The Wet or The Dry, this was an extremely harsh part of the world.

'Which one of the girls is Karlee?' she asked. 'I still can't get a handle on what name goes with what kid.'

'She's the real feisty one who talks ten to the dozen without drawing breath.'

'I repeat my question, Parish. That answer is too generic!'

He laughed. 'She's the third one. Which coincidently leads us to the fifth and final muster camp, known as Number Three, because it's usually the third one mustered.'

Gina fought a grin. 'That sounds so convoluted I'm not sure if I should believe you or not.'

'Scout's honour. Would I lie to you?' His voice had a theatrically wounded tone.

'I don't know you well enough to be certain.'

There was a moment's pause before he responded.

'Maybe it's time you took a couple of chances, Gina...like trusting me and getting to know me better.'

His voice had dropped to a suggestive, sensual whisper that sent tingles of temptation through Gina's body. She had to put her left hand over her right to minimize the tremble and keep the microphone steady as she responded.

'I've never approved of gambling, Parish. I learned early on that I wanted my life to be organized, predictable and practical. Taking chances results in false hopes, short-term thrills and pain.' She released the transmit button and drew a much-needed breath.

'You know, Gina, holding false hopes is much more positive than having no hope at all. And as far as I can tell, the only time a person is immune to pain is when they're so full of booze they can't feel anything.'

There was a long silence. Finally Gina broke it.

'I notice you couldn't gloss over my aversion to short-term thrills.'

'I wasn't trying to gloss over anything, Gina,' he responded softly. 'I was being honest.' There was a longish pause before he continued. 'To me a thrill has to be short term. A thing loses its excitement and freshness once it develops longevity. When that happens it's simply a nice, familiar habit.'

Like regular, adequate sex in a bed with your fiancé, Gina thought miserably. Then she realized that at least the circumstances of her relationship with James hadn't left her fighting to recover from it. There was nothing wrong with the nice and familiar. It made for peace of mind.

'Listen to me, Gina,' Parish said, as if he could actually see her distraction. 'It's late, and we're both tired, so this probably isn't a good time for us to get into this. I'll call you tomorrow night, okay?'

Taking a deep, cleansing breath, Gina depressed the button on her handset. 'No. Don't call me, Parish. Not anymore. Not unless it's business or an emergency.'

Before he could respond she switched off the radio. She knew she was a coward, but she couldn't do sex without a safety net, not with a man like Parish Dunford.

Not when she was predisposed to repeat her mother's mistake of allowing her heart to rule her head.

CHAPTER NINE

THE next few days were agonizingly long and slow. Gina blamed it on the heat, the silence, the government's foreign debt…

Sunday was even longer, yet he still didn't make it home.

Monday she'd made coffee and was in front of the computer by the time the sun had fully risen, filled with both apprehension and anticipation.

By eleven o'clock the coffee was cold, the screen saver had activated from lack of use, and nervous tension had replaced the blood flowing through Gina's veins. And he *still* wasn't back.

A little after midday, her lungs and heart collided as they simultaneously leapt into her throat at the sound of an engine outside. She was out of her chair and at the office door before her overt eagerness registered. Bracing her hands against the doorjamb, she fought to regain her composure. Dear God, she was practically trembling!

'Gina! You in the office? Gina!'

Her heart sunk as Leanne's voice carried from the back door. For a moment she sagged against the wall. 'I…I'm coming.'

As she made her way to the kitchen, she forced a smile, but she knew it wouldn't hold a candle to the beaming expression on Leanne's face.

'They're back!' she announced excitedly. 'Rusty just called. They're down at the bullock paddock, and he reckons they'll be through in a couple of hours. But I can't wait that long to see him so I'm gonna drive down there. You wanna come?'

A couple of weeks ago she'd have said *no, thanks* without a moment's hesitation, but now her curiosity about life on a cattle property had grown considerably. Of course, Parish had offered to take her to a muster camp, but would the offer still hold? Or would the comment she'd made when they'd last spoken about only wanting to deal with him in a business capacity negate it? If so, this might be the only opportunity she would get to see something of what mustering entailed, and from the point of view of her job, it could only be advantageous to see a practical part of mustering.

Oh, who was she trying to kid? It wasn't the mustering she was curious about. It was Parish! And there was nothing businesslike about her motives.

'Gina?'

'Oh, sorry, Leanne.' She smiled. 'Thanks anyway, but it might be better if I don't go. I've…I've been at the computer all morning, but I have nothing to show for it.' Wasn't that the truth! 'I think I'd better stay here and—'

'Hey, a break will do you good! Clear the mind and all that stuff! Crikey, you've been working so hard I haven't seen you for days!'

Working hard—yeah, right! More like mooning around like a lovesick moron! Maybe the best thing she could do was expose herself to a good strong dose of *reality* instead of getting caught up in her fantasies. Because that's what she'd been doing. Allowing dreams—where a tuxedoed Parish accompanied her to plays and elegant dinners and made soft gentle love to her in her white on white bedroom—to contaminate her better judgment.

Well, reality check! Parish wasn't the type for plays and dinner parties. He probably didn't *own* a tuxedo, and even if he did he'd no doubt wear his spurs and beat-up Akubra with it! Plus, there was no way a wide-awake woman could look at Parish Dunford and equate him with soft, gentle anything! And the *very* last thing she needed to be doing was visualizing herself in a relationship that dressed sex up as *love*making!

'You're right, Leanne,' she said. 'I do need to clear my head. Desperately.'

It was Parish's theory that getting a mob of cattle to file through gates into a holding paddock or yard in an orderly manner at first try was every ringer's ultimate goal. To date he'd never seen it happen, and he quickly realized today wasn't going to change things, as the leaders gathered in a tight huddle, refusing to move. Their continuous groan of protest was broken only by the crack of stockwhips and curses of the men wheeling their mounts at high speed in an effort to get the upper hand. Everything was going on within a cloud of hoof-stirred dust that seemed as thick in the air and a bloke's mouth as it did on the ground.

He was using the weight of his horse to guide yet another wayward beast in the right direction when his peripheral vision caught a near collision between two of his ringers. He cursed, knowing that to persist with what they were doing with visibility this bad was an unnecessary risk to both horses and riders. Pulling to the fringe of the melee with the intention of locating Rusty and telling him he was riding tail on the herd and they were switching tactics, he spotted the station Jeep and the two women sitting on the bonnet.

'Hell! Like I don't have enough flamin' problems!'

'Now what are they doing?' Gina spoke through clamped teeth in a bid to minimize her dust diet.

'Turning them back from the gate,' Leanne replied. 'What they'll do is cut a smaller more manageable mob from the herd and drive them into the paddock. The theory being that once they see their mates in there, the rest of the mob will be more agreeable about going in.'

'And if that doesn't work?'

'Then it'll be a longer day than anyone wants. Oh, look, here comes Parish!'

Oh, my God! Gina thought with immediate dread. But, as her gaze followed the direction of the other woman's, the same thought repeated itself as a more reverent, *Oh...my...God...*

The sight of Parish astride the huge grey horse galloping towards them was nothing short of breathtakingly magnificent and heartstoppingly masculine. Atop the animal he seemed larger than life, and there was something almost sensual about the way his body harmonized with the motion of the horse, as if they were one. The nearer he came, the closer Gina felt to visceral meltdown. How could a man look that damned good, no, *wonderful*, covered in dust and damp with sweat?

'If you weren't pregnant, Lee,' he said, reining in the horse, 'I'd ask you to saddle up one of the spare horses and help out.'

'If I wasn't pregnant, I wouldn't give you time to ask!' she retorted, looking longingly at the working ringers. 'I'd give my right arm to be out there.'

'Hey, I'd give my right *and* my left to have you there.'

'That'd make it just like the old days, when I had to do my work plus yours!'

Parish's grin though not aimed in Gina's direction, was no less potent than if it had been. Her pulse skittered all over the place, and she felt as if someone had lit a sparkler in her lower abdomen.

'Seen Rusty yet?' Once again Parish looked directly at Leanne, nothing in his manner indicating he was even aware of the presence of a third person, and Gina had to bite her tongue to keep from saying, *Have I vanished into thin air or what*?

'Only to wave to,' Leanne replied. 'He was working flat out. Looks to me like we could've done with a few more ringers.'

'What muster couldn't?' he asked, his attention on the inside of the Jeep. 'Where are the kids?'

'Taking a nap at home, with Snake baby-sitting.'

'Geez, that sounds dangerous.'

'For Snake or the kids?' Gina asked dryly. There was no reaction of shock to confirm her fear of invisibility. Indeed, had it not been for his disinterested shrug, she'd have suspected her voice no longer existed, either.

At that moment, the approach of another rider drew a cry of delight from Leanne. She slid awkwardly from the bonnet of the Jeep, practically dancing with excitement until Rusty dismounted, then raced into his arms to be thoroughly hugged and kissed. Turning from the pair with what she refused to label as envy, Gina fixed her gaze on the antics of the cattle and other ringers.

'I take it your presence here means you've got some business problem that couldn't wait until I got home?'

She quickly glanced over both her shoulders. 'Are you talking to *me*?' she asked, pointing to herself.

'I'm too busy for games, Gina. Why are you here instead of bent over the computer?'

'I'm on my lunchbreak!' she adlibbed, then added, 'but I can assure you I haven't been neglecting my job in your absence.'

'Good. Because I expect to be brought up to date on everything you've accomplished so far.'

'No problem!'

'Fine, then expect to see me in the office when I get back to the homestead.'

She opened her mouth to say something witty, but whatever it was evaporated under hot speculation about how his rough, unshaved jaw would feel beneath her fingers...against *her* jaw...against...

'Some of us can't afford the luxury of a lunchbreak.'

The gruffness of his voice jolted her.

'So *I'll* be getting back to work now,' he said. 'Try not to be too long doing the same thing.'

'Try not to fall off your high horse,' she muttered to his departing form. 'From that lofty altitude, Parish Dunford, you'd leave a crater the size of your ego!'

By the time all the cattle were secured in the bullock paddock, Parish was the only man wishing the task had taken longer. While the rest of them had been eagerly spouting on about what they were going to do over the next four days, he'd been thinking of ways to delay his return to the homestead.

Telling Gina he wanted to go over the work she'd been doing for him hadn't been smart. It'd been a spur-of-the-moment comment, a way of reinforcing that he could be as business-oriented about their relationship as she could. The trouble was, it was more for his benefit than hers, because he knew damned well he was more interested in a computer programmer than he'd ever been in computers. Not once in his life had he sat astride a horse and avoided looking at a computer because its mere presence had turned him hot and hard in the saddle.

'Hey, Parish, where're you headin'?' Rusty asked when he didn't turn towards the house as he left the tack room.

'Down the swimming hole.'

The look Rusty sent him was no less incredulous than he'd expected. Rusty knew Parish's routine immediately after a muster was to grab a beer, a shower and sleep, the length of the sleep being the only variation from his daily routine. Not in fifteen years had he even *thought* of breaking it, much less announced his intentions. That he was doing so now to take a swim after a week of bathing in creek water so hard it couldn't even raise a decent lather from shampoo, much less soap, by rights shouldn't have had Rusty slack-jawed with amazement, but yelling for the men in white coats. Had he known Parish intended to *walk* the kilometre and a half rather than ride or take one of the station vehicles, he'd have probably shot him on the spot simply for everyone else's safety.

But Parish was prepared to have Rusty think he'd lost his mind rather than risk what scant sanity he might still possess for the sake of an immediate beer and a hot shower. While he could probably make the trip to the refrigerator without any problem, phases two and three of his routine required walking past his office. Walking past a room that contained the one thing that had occupied his mind nonstop for the past week, past a woman he wanted to possess with a need that challenged his self-control to breaking point.

Parish decided that while discretion might be widely advertised as the better part of valour, procrastination, at least in this instance, represented the remainder, and was a better option. Because it was going to be damned hard to keep things discreet when his first instincts were to back Gina Petrocelli up against a wall and kiss her senseless.

To anyone passing the office, it would've looked like Gina was hard at work over the computer dealing with Malagara's records. In actual fact she was dropping bombs with lethal accuracy on an alien creature who dissolved into a murky green puddle before vanishing from the screen. She'd named the creature P.D., because invariably it kept reappearing to distract her from her galactic mission. It was a tenacious and irritating creature. She was scanning the screen in anticipation of its odious return when she heard the back door slam. Instantly her hand stilled on the control.

The familiar sound of booted feet and the tinkle of spurs proclaimed her reprieve over. Symbolically, the alien stealthily reappeared and blew her spaceship off the computerized planet.

Loser! Want to play again? the smirking creature asked via a caption bubble.

'Like I need you *and* your human counterpart,' she muttered, hitting the escape key.

With deft fingers, she brought up the main menu for the Malagara program. She didn't need to look away from the screen to know Parish was propped in the doorway off to her left—her body's response was more than enough to confirm his proximity. Determined to ignore her shallow and wanton body, she spoke in a flat, disinterested voice.

'So you're back?'

'And I thought you were just a pretty face!'

She turned, intending to glare at his facetious tone, but it took all her effort not to gasp out loud at the sight of him. She didn't know if she was more awed, shocked or fascinated by his state of semi-undress, but she couldn't help being appreciative of what she saw.

The shirtless Parish displayed the most perfect masculine chest she'd ever seen outside of a male centrefold or a jeans commercial. Actually, if she'd had a camera she'd have had the means of launching him in a whole new career as a male model. Then again, if her own erratic heart rate was any indication, a public exposé of masculinity this potent would put millions of women at risk of cardiac arrest.

He was sipping casually on a beer and made no move to continue down the hall or enter the room—*thank God*! If he got any closer she'd probably hyperventilate! Swallowing hard, she tried to conceal the extent of his impact on her.

'Was there something you wanted, Parish?'

A muscle jerked at the side of his mouth before he said, 'Only to see if you were ready to give me a run-down on what you've been doing.'

'Right now?'

He shrugged. The absence of a shirt made the action way too provocative. 'Sure, why not? Is that a problem for you?'

'Um…don't you want to take a shower first?'

He shook his head. 'I've just had a swim.'

'Oh.' She supposed that explained the lack of a shirt, but it didn't solve her problem. 'Um, maybe you should change anyway,' she suggested. 'Your jeans are thick with dust, and…and computers shouldn't be exposed to dust.'

An amused smirk that hinted at perfect white teeth momentarily lured her eyes from his chest. 'Then I'll try not to expose the computer to my legs.'

As he spoke, those long, dusty, denim-clad limbs began moving into the room, creating feelings within Gina that had her wondering if she wasn't perhaps claustrophobic.

'I…I really do think it'd be better to do this when you weren't drinking beer.'

Parish didn't miss the snobby, disapproving tone she injected into the words. He hadn't heard her use it since those first couple of days of her arrival, but now it grated like hell with him.

'I can drink and watch at the same time.' Defiantly he lifted the can to his mouth while keeping his eyes on her.

'I'm sure you can. Nevertheless I'd prefer you didn't.'

For several seconds Parish considered simply turning on his heel and walking out. It would have been the smart thing to do, but it was also exactly what she wanted him to do. Smiling, he crushed the can in one hand and tossed it into the wastepaper basket at the end of the desk. 'There you go, teacher. I'm ready to start the lesson. How about you?'

'Yes, I'm ready.' She looked flustered as she scrambled to her feet and nudged the chair towards him. 'But I'd appreciate it if you'd stop being flippant, Parish, and just sit down and concentrate on what I'm trying to teach you.'

He was tempted to say that thanks to her he wouldn't have a hope of concentrating on anything ever again! 'Where will you sit?'

'I'll stand behind you. I always stand when I'm training someone.'

He sat down, enjoying the perfumed scent of her as she stood next to him.

'As I told you before,' she went on, repositioning things on the desk and not looking at him, 'this is a top of the range computer. It has everything from an adjustable keyboard, which…'

She could have been speaking Latin with a Russian accent for all the sense her words made to Parish as she rattled on about RAM, bytes, hard drives, response and downloading capacity, but he wasn't in any hurry to shut her up. Her preoccupation with the computer was giving him the opportunity to indulge his own fascination with her. Slowly he let his gaze slide over every delicious curve she possessed, from the tip of her thick lustrous hair to her bare, pink-toenailed feet.

The denim shorts she wore were just that—*short*. They moulded her hips and magnificently taut bottom like a second skin, and the thought of what she'd look and *feel* like in nothing but her first skin caused his teeth to sweat. In contrast, her unrevealing white sleeveless shirt was more subtle, but nonetheless the buttons and knotted tails at the waist were a nerve-racking temptation that had his fingers itching.

'I'm sure you'll agree once you get some hands-on experience.'

Parish's body jolted his brain back to life. *She couldn't have said what he thought she had*!

'What did you say?'

She sighed and glared at him. 'You haven't been listening to a word I've said, have you?'

'Sorry, my mind was on other things.' Knowing his life expectancy would be under threat if he told her *what other things*, he offered an apologetic smile.

'It's supposed,' she said tersely, 'to be on *me* and what I'm telling you.'

He grinned. 'Do I get points for being half right?'

*   *   *

Gina was sure the room tilted onto an angle but wasn't certain if it was because of his smile or what he'd said. While she was trying to analyse the exact cause, Parish began to fiddle with the computer.

'This is called a mouse, right?' he asked, picking up the object in question.

'Um…yeah. You use it to—'

'Get into files and stuff instead of the keyboard,' he finished smugly. 'And this little thing moves the cursor backwards and forwards or up and down on the screen.' He was gliding his thumb over the ball at the back of the mouse in a slow, suggestive manner and spoke in a similarly hypnotic tone.

'Parish!' she squealed, leaping away when he unexpectedly ran it up her thigh.

His expression was unrepentant. 'A typical female reaction to a mouse. Guess that's how it got the name, huh?' he said, watching her as he began to again finger the roller.

She snatched it from him. 'Don't do that!'

'Why not?'

'Because…because you'll stuff the roller!'

'Sorry, I'm not conversant with the technical intricacies of computer bits and pieces. I should probably stick with what I know.'

Gina gasped as he pulled her onto his lap and ran his hand over her thigh. 'Parish! What are—'

His mouth prevented her from completing what would've been a really dumb question. She knew precisely what he was doing and hastily lifted her arms to his neck to prevent him from changing his mind.

By rights she should have been repelled by the prickliness of his unshaved jaw and the taste of beer, but she wasn't. Instead her entire body seemed energized by his blatant, raw masculinity and the unexpected gentleness with which his tongue sought entry to her mouth. When she granted it, they sighed as one and instinctively pressed closer to each other.

For Gina, hearing the unison of their relief made her tingle, for it meant she wasn't alone in her desire. Parish wanted her every bit as much as she wanted him. She'd thought the notion was unbelievably arousing, but it was nothing compared to the sensations that erupted within her as he repositioned her leg so that she was straddling him. Slow heat spiralled through her as he held her hips and hauled her hard against his denim-covered erection.

'Tell me!' he rasped against her throat.

He'd asked the question with actions, not words, and she elected to reply in the same way. Dragging his mouth back to hers, she rotated her hips and nuzzled more firmly into his lap.

Half a heartbeat later they were on the floor, Gina willingly surrendering herself to a passion she'd previously defeated with denial as clothes were peeled away with ravenous haste....

CHAPTER TEN

LOOKING down on her naked beauty, Parish couldn't decide what he found most incredible, the sheer physical perfection of her body or the sultry passion burning in her liquid brown eyes. He got no clue from the tremble of his hands as he lowered them to her bare breasts for the first time, for that might just as easily have been caused by pent-up anticipation or the sensual pout of her lips as she arched towards his touch. Or perhaps by the almost raw terror he felt at the knowledge that making love with this woman wasn't the way to get her out of his system, yet even if that was the cause of his almost virginal awe, it would've taken a bullet to the heart to stop him now.

Beneath his hands her skin felt like warmed silk... sensuous, soft and exotic. Beneath his tongue her beaded nipples tasted like honey-dipped pearls... hard and deliciously sweet. And to his ears, her moans of pleasure were the echo of his own. He wanted to be gentle with her to cherish the newness of the emotions and sensations she aroused within him, but he wasn't sure how long his control would last. Never had he wanted a woman as desperately or completely as he wanted this one.

Gina gave up mentally trying to identify the thousands of sensations bombarding her body and soul and focused only on experiencing them... and Parish. Her senses were awash with him, his earthy masculine scent, the salty taste of his skin as their passion raised a sweat, the guttural groans of pleasure he emitted as her hands traced the sculptured hardness of his muscular body, the erotic delights his calloused hands and fingers triggered within her.

She whimpered with pleasure as he suckled on her nipples, his oral expertise creating miniature electric shocks deep in her loins, frissons of excitement that left her moist and aching with a hunger she'd never known. The uniqueness of what she was feeling was as terrifying as it was exciting, and instinctively she touched him to convey her needs. He bucked in reaction, his head lifting and his blue eyes locking with hers for several seconds before closing again as his jaw tensed with the strain of holding on to his self-control. Caught in momentary smugness at her ability to affect this man as intensely as he did her, she was unprepared for the swiftness and ease with which he grasped her wrist and freed himself from her.

Now it was she who was trapped, her arms pinned above her head.

Parish saw no sign of fear in her face. In fact, her smile was seduction itself as he lowered his mouth to it. Her eager tongue and muted murmurs revealed her passion was flaming as high as his own, and transferring her pinned hands into one of his, he used his free one to both temporarily placate and elevate her sexual needs. But he discovered power was a two-edged blade, for she rode his hand with a wanton enthusiasm that came close to sending him over the edge.

'You, Parish,' she moaned, 'I want *you*!'

Instantly he began to lower himself over her, but her hands went to his shoulder, and understanding what she wanted he rolled onto his back.

She smiled as she mounted him and in that millisecond of time, even before their unified gasp of pleasure bounced off the walls, Parish knew he was in love. He knew it. Without any hint. Without any forewarning. Without a doubt. Just like that, he knew.

Parish Dunford was in love with Gina Petrocelli.

Yet before he had a chance to admit as much, she'd stretched her body over his and claimed his mouth. Once that happened his mind lost all ability to function.

Gina knew her last-ditch effort to stay in control was shot to hell the moment she and Parish united as one. Beyond that point all she knew was the most phenomenal bliss....

The air in the small office was still thick with the residual scent of passion, though the gasped cries of ecstasy and subsequent pants of exhaustion had receded. Gina lay atop Parish, her head on his shoulder with her face turned from him. She was only dimly aware of his arm across the small of her back that prevented her sweaty body from sliding from his, and the gentleness of his hand as he stroked her hair, for her attention was turned inwards as she stared at his carelessly discarded jeans and the leather belt looped through them.

The silver belt buckle was embossed with the image of a rider trying to tame a bucking horse, its surface dulled somewhat by fine scratches that came from regular, indifferent wear. Gina wished she knew if the rider depicted on the buckle had triumphed over the horse or if he'd fallen to earth, the battered loser in the contest, for in the aftermath of an experience she'd craved beyond the wisdom of self-denial, Gina saw parallels between herself and that rider. She, too, had believed she could take control and emerge unscathed from a situation common sense told her was a risk. In the wake of the most emotional ride of her life, it would've been comforting to know with certainty that the silver-moulded rider had walked away without any permanent scars.

'You okay?' Parish's question was a gentle whisper that grazed her bare shoulder, yet pierced her heart.

'Okay?' She laughed softly. 'If I say yes I'd be guilty of aiding and abetting you in massive understatement.' She allowed him to turn her head.

'If I'm understating things it's only because my brain's too stunned to function.' His eyes roamed her face with a kind of bemused appreciation. 'I had a gut feeling we'd be good together, Gina,' he said. 'But that went beyond good sex.'

'The bliss of simultaneous climax.' She sighed. 'I read once where it was reputed to be something of a rarity.'

He traced her lips, a small smile playing on his own. 'Is that a veiled challenge to me to try and repeat what just happened?'

Shaking her head, she rolled off him to lie in the crook of his arm. The motion of separation from his body brought an instant chill to hers. She made no attempt to resist him as he cuddled her closer. 'It's simply an explanation of what was for me the best sex of my life.'

Parish tensed at her description. 'The best *sex* of your life?'

'Yeah.' She grinned at him. 'You're going to be a hard act to follow, Parish Dunford.'

'But you intend to try anyway?'

She sat up, manoeuvring onto her knees and turning her back towards him as she reached for her shirt. 'Don't get all bent out of shape,' she said, turning the garment right side out. 'I was paying you a compliment.'

'I'm not looking for compliments, damn you! Are you telling me that to you what happened to us was simply sex?'

'Yes,' she said. 'We scarcely know each other, so it's ridiculous to pretend otherwise.'

'Bull, Gina. There was more to it than sex, and you know it! We connected on an *emotional* level, not just a physical level.'

Her shoulders heaved under the weight of her sigh before she pulled on her shirt. 'We experienced a simultaneous climax. It momentarily distorted our thinking, that's all.'

'Our thinking was distorted long before that. We didn't use a condom.' Swearing, she spun to face him. 'Relax, Gina, the worst thing I could give you is a baby.'

Her relief was visible. 'Ditto here.' A self-conscious half smile tugged at her mouth. 'You mightn't have been my first lover, but you're the only one who's been *entirely* naked. Hey!' she exclaimed, the tiny smile becoming a grin. 'No condom! *That's* probably the reason it was so good!'

Parish limited himself to a noncommittal shrug. He knew otherwise, but given Gina's delight in the conclusion she'd drawn, it was obvious she found the possibility a huge relief. He didn't have to be a genius to figure out Gina Petrocelli needed a tangible explanation for the extravagant bliss they'd just experienced. She didn't want to consider that a strong emotional connection was responsible for the exquisite quality of their lovemaking. Why?

The probable answer to that rocked him.

'Gina...are you involved with a bloke in Sydney? Is that why you're so eager to...you know, play this down?'

Thick-lashed brown eyes flashed with fury. 'I can't believe you asked that! Of course I'm not involved with anyone! If I was, this wouldn't have happened! You think I'd just go around...'

His joy was so great it immunized him against her anger, and undaunted, he grabbed one of her furiously waving arms and dragged her across his chest. Usually he enjoyed competition, but in this particular case he was more than grateful to have the whole track to himself.

'Lemme go!' she demanded, wriggling furiously.

'Nope! I've decided to do my own research on the rarity of the simultaneous climax.'

She shoved her long dark hair from her face to glare at him. 'That'll be tough to do on your own!'

'That's why I've chosen you as a volunteer. Pleased?'

'No, I'm damned well not!'

'Yeah, you are.... You're just scared witless that I'm right. That regardless of whether we come simultaneously or not, we're better together than any other two people on the planet.' He smiled. 'Admit it.'

Gina dearly wished she'd pulled her knickers on under her shirt, because it wasn't easy to act morally outraged with a guy whose hands were delivering the most delightful massage to your naked buttocks. And especially when said guy was also looking at you with eyes hot enough to melt your bones. Little by little she felt her reluctance to repeat what had happened between them being drowned by an obsessive need to do exactly that.

'Parish,' she said weakly as his other hand directed her head down towards his. 'I…I…' Whatever she was going to say was absorbed by his mouth, and all recollection of it was wiped from her mind with just one taste of him. She felt her anger dissolve and her limbs turn leaden as Parish's lips and hands persisted in working their magic. Kissing this man was as soothing as it was stimulating, blurring the distinction between being sensually relaxed and inflamed with desire.

'I think…' Parish said, when breathlessness forced them to part. 'It's time…to head to the…bedroom.' Unable to help himself, he lifted a hand and laid it against her flawless cheek. Just her smile as she rubbed her face against his palm touched him in a way no one else ever had, never would.

'Your place or mine?' she teased, as he pulled her to her feet.

'Doesn't matter, s'long as this time we get to make love in a bed.'

'Have *sex* in a bed.'

Parish thought her correction sounded more automatic than sincere. 'Sure, sweetheart,' he said, fighting a smug grin as he swept her into his arms. 'Whatever you say.'

Parish was in the blissful state of semi-awakeness when the warm, pliant woman in his arms let loose with a common four-letter description of what he himself had been contemplating and leapt out of his arms and the bed.

Simultaneously! a cynical little voice inside him noted.

'We slept in! I'm late taking it!' Sweeping the Doona from the bed, Gina scampered across the room trying to drape it over her nudity.

'Late taking…' He let the question die as she moved like greased lightening into the hall.

Squinting against the invasive sunlight streaming in the window, he flopped back against the pillow for several moments before turning his head to glance at the clock on the nightstand. Twenty to nine. By rights he ought to get up, take a shower and get dressed. He grinned at the pleasant dilemma that exercise would create.

'Any reason why you're lying there grinning like an idiot at the ceiling?' Gina asked.

He widened his smile. 'Drop the bedspread and I'll tell you.'

She laughed, looking so damn beautiful it almost sucked the air from his lungs.

'You always fly out of bed like a dislodged bronc buster?'

'God, I love it when you talk dirty!'

'So come back to bed and prepare yourself for the unabridged, uncensored version of my life.'

She shook her head. 'I've got work to do.'

'No, you don't. I'm giving you the day off.' He patted the mattress. 'C'mere.'

Only the slightest hint of hesitation showed on her face before she sauntered across the room and flopped stomach first onto the bed. And there wasn't the slightest resistance from her when he caught her to him and kissed her.

'Good morning, Gina,' he said solemnly.

She smiled. 'Good morning to you, too.'

'Now would you like to explain why you bolted out of

here a few moments ago like someone put a hot branding iron on your flank?'

'I had to take my pill.'

He frowned. 'What, the one that stops you from dissolving in daylight?'

She punched his arm. 'The one that stops me turning into a balloon and producing a screaming infant. *The* pill.'

'So? Why the drama? I mean, as long as you take it daily you're safe, right?' That's what he'd always assumed.

'More or less, but ideally you should take them at roughly the same time of day.'

'And that makes it more effective?'

She shrugged. 'All I know is I've taken mine at seven-thirty, *religiously*, for eight years, and I'm not anxious to jeopardize a hundred percent success rate now. What's the frown for?'

'Well, being a male, I'm not real up on the subject, but isn't continuous long-term use of the pill bad? Doesn't it mess up a woman's fertility and stuff?'

'Parish,' she said. 'That's the whole idea of taking it.'

He scowled at her deliberately patronizing tone. 'What I mean is what if when you *want* to have kids you find you have trouble getting pregnant?'

'Well, some women might consider that a problem, but *I'm* not one of them. I don't want kids.'

'Not ever?'

'Nope. Well, at least not in the plural sense. I've more or less decided that if I married a guy who was *really* into kids I might consider having one,' she conceded in such an emotionless tone, Parish was tempted to check to see if she still had a pulse.

'You've more or less decided you might consider having one?' he repeated.

'Mmm. Preferably a girl. Because that way, if the guy bailed out on his Daddy duties, I wouldn't be forced to endure hours on the sidelines watching macho sports I have no interest in or camping out in primitive conditions in order to ensure the child had a balanced exposure to guy things.' Her tone was painfully matter-of-fact.

'I think kids should only be brought into an extremely stable, financially secure marriage that's been structured with them in mind,' she continued. 'I have a real problem with people becoming parents, especially multiple parents, because of a slack attitude to birth control or because they think it's their right or because little Johnny needs a play-mate.'

Gina realized that Parish was looking at her as if she'd just grown a second head. She sighed. It was hardly a big surprise. 'You're the type of guy who works on the more the merrier theory. Don't deny it,' she said when he went to open his mouth. 'The expression on your face says it all.'

'Actually, I'm trying to work out whether you don't like kids, are some sort of rabid radical supporter of them, or you're trying to convert me to zero population growth.'

Gina smiled. 'I don't dislike kids, I'm just not crazy about what raising them entails. Which,' she said, 'is why, if I ever did decide to do it, I'd definitely limit the exercise to one.' She flicked her hair out of the way and stared at him. 'Believe me, Parish, I'm completely uninspired by the so-called joys of round-the-clock child care.'

On the rare occasions Parish had thought about marriage and his future, he'd always pictured himself with a mini-mum of three kids, with sons outnumbering daughters and a doting albeit faceless wife who devoted herself entirely to him and their kids. It wasn't something he thought about a lot, but when he did the basic scenario was always pretty much the same.

What's more, he'd always figured that once he found the woman he wanted to spend the rest of his life with she'd share all the same dreams for the future he did. News flash! He'd figured wrong. Nothing Gina had said matched up with anything he'd imagined. Although there *was* one thing she'd omitted to mention.

'Ah, assuming you did find yourself in a perfectly structured marriage with a bloke who was, um, *into kids*, and you decided to have one—*preferably a girl*,' he added. 'Would you give up your career to be a full-time mother?'

'Of course not!' She looked horrified. 'My God, that'd be the worst thing I could do to the child!'

He blinked. 'It would?'

'Of course it would, Parish! I'd be totally miserable with nothing to challenge my brain. The whole thing would be a disaster! I'd start resenting both husband and child, not to mention lose all self-esteem into the bargain! The marriage would fall apart, everyone would endure a messy divorce and I'd end up an unemployed single parent bitter with the world!'

Her face was alive with indignation, but despite all the differences she'd highlighted between them, Parish knew he'd never be satisfied with anyone else.

'I'm not cut out for the idealized picture of domesticity, Parish,' she said in a calmer voice. 'I value my independence and my personal space too much.'

'I see. Well, in that case we've got a real problem on our hands.'

His eyes darkened to almost navy, and he watched her with an intensity that set off tiny internal alarms in Gina. Rising to her knees, impeded by the cocoon of the Doona, she began to back away, sensing he was about to say something deep and meaningful she didn't want to hear.

'Parish, I think I know what you're going to say, but…' Just as she was about to slip off the bed, he snared her wrist.

'*Please, Parish…*' Her voice was pleading, but she didn't try to tug free. 'I don't want to discuss problems. Not this morning…not now. I just want to have a shower and—'

'I know. That's the problem.' He winked. 'So do I.'

For a moment her face was completely and beautifully blank, then understanding dawned in the form of a wide, sexy smile. It took Parish no time at all to unwrap her and kiss it from her mouth....

Gina prided herself on never being one to skirt the facts, and the fact was, she *knew* she was tempting fate by having an affair with Parish. However, she reasoned, as long as she was prepared to face that fact and accept it, then there was no real harm in a little bit of light-hearted, physical self-indulgence. In a little over three days, Parish would leave on the second muster, which would take five weeks, so by the time he returned, she'd be back in Sydney, re-entrenched in the lifestyle she'd always wanted and was thoroughly happy with.

Their short-lived relationship would be over. It would exist only in their memories and personal histories.

There was no reason to fear any long-term repercussions by taking a slight detour from her carefully mapped out path to the future, she told herself. Her fling with Parish was nothing more than the equivalent of a teenage girl's rebellious romance with a bad boy from the wrong side of the tracks. And since as a teenager she'd been so agog at suddenly landing on the right side of the tracks that rebellion had been a missed opportunity, technically she was overdue for a hot, torrid affair that ran against convention, even her own conventions.

Parish watched in silence as Gina competently put her horse through a series of neat figure eights in the horse-breaking yard. When he'd suggested they take a ride, he'd expected her to be a complete novice and had wanted to get some idea of how confident she was going to be once they got into open ground. Though her riding style was proof she'd learned the skill at a posh pony club, she had a good seat

and didn't fight the horse with the reins as if she was trying
to land an oversized fish. Not that she'd need to with any
of his horses. They were all beautifully soft-mouthed and
responsive.

'That's enough, smartie!' he said wryly. 'Why didn't you
tell me you could ride?'

Smug amusement lit her face. 'You never asked.'

'True, but if you'd said something, I'd have made a horse
available and you could've been riding every day.'

She shrugged. 'I suppose so. But to be truthful I didn't
give it a thought. I haven't been on a horse since I turned
seventeen.'

Parish swung himself onto his own horse. 'In that case
we'd better keep this short, or you'll wind up too sore to
sit down tonight.'

Nudging her horse towards the gate, she shot him a
pointed look. 'Call me cynical,' she said. 'But I suspect it
isn't the possibility of me not being able to sit down that
you're really worried about.'

'You're cynical! The thought of sex never entered my
mind!'

'Really? That's strange. I can't get it out of mine!'
Laughing, she jammed her heels into her mount and took
off in a canter.

'Beautiful, isn't it?' Parish asked her as she brought her
horse to a halt and sat silently scanning their surroundings.

Gina whispered her reply, because in the tranquillity of
the area, a raised voice would've been like screeching obscenities in a church. 'Very beautiful.'

Majestic green trees formed huge areas of shade along
the banks of a creek so clear it was possible to count the
pebbles scattered across its bottom in sections. In others the
sunshine reflected off the glassy surface, creating a visually
impenetrable barrier of glare. Motioning her horse forward
a few steps, she stood in her stirrups and touched the foliage.

'What sort of tree is this?' she asked, the leaves' softness striking her as being in keeping with the gentle beauty of the scene to which they belonged.

'A coolibah,' Parish said from behind her. 'But it's not a real good idea to go about grabbing hold of leaves out here. Some trees will give you a nasty surprise.'

She turned in the saddle. 'Such as?'

Parish dismounted and motioned for her to do the same. 'The leaves of the Parkinsonia, which like the coolibah grows along river and creek banks, have tiny little hooks on them.'

She surrendered her reins into his hand and watched as he tied the horses to a branch. It seemed the most natural thing in the world that when he completed the task he linked his fingers through hers and she fell into stride with him as he started walking along the water's edge.

'Riding through Parkinsonia,' he continued, 'can be a damn prickly experience. Mimosa is even more vicious.'

'Why's that?' she asked, more to hear the sound of his voice than out of any great botanical interest.

'It's a bush, sort of like a briar, with long, sharp thorns. Blue came back from the muster carrying a healthy dose of scratches from it.'

'What happened?'

'It was dark, we were working late, cutting calves from a small mob, and Blue was working the face of the camp and—'

'The face of the camp?' she repeated, stopping dead and giving him a droll look. 'Parish, I don't understand a word of what that means. Do you think you could remember you're dealing with an ignorant city slicker here?'

He grinned, tilting her chin up with one finger to drop a quick kiss on her lips. 'Well, now you know how I feel when you slip into high-tech computer jargon. To a dumb bushie like me, ram capacity relates to the stud potential of a sheep.'

She jerked his hat right down over his eyes. 'Dumb bushie, my eye! You can't fool me, Parish Dunford, I've *seen* the figures for Dunford Downs.'

'My grandfather was responsible for building up the Downs. The credit for its success goes to him.'

'But you've run it since his death. *And* with a massively increased profit margin.'

He shrugged. 'I've been lucky so far, but that doesn't guarantee the future. Continued success in this business relies as much on the climate being kind to you as it does on managerial skills...probably more. A couple of years of drought can leave you with a lot of dead cattle and the seat out of your pants.'

A distant but gentle expression came into his eyes. 'My grandfather used to say that every year a grazier stayed on the land he was gambling with God.'

'But if the future of Dunford Downs is so...I don't know...*uncertain*, why did you buy Malagara. Why double your risk?'

'Because the Downs was my grandfather's dream, and I want my own.'

'Haven't you ever wanted to do anything else with your life besides raise cattle?'

'Nope.'

He answered without the slightest hesitation—just as Gina had feared he would. Like her, he had his life indelibly mapped out without room for compromise. It was what all sensible people did.

Why, then, did she feel more miserable than sensible?

CHAPTER ELEVEN

GINA'S heart was in her mouth as she watched the glossy black colt fight to dislodge Parish from his back. Time and time again as the animal bucked, then gyrated in midair, she was torn between the urge to shut her eyes, fearing Parish would come crashing to the ground, and keeping them open so she didn't miss a solitary second of the magnificent battle between man and beast.

Around her the air was dense with dust thrown up by the colt's aggressive antics, and twice she'd hastily leapt backwards from her standing position on the bottom cross rail of the yard fence when it lunged in her direction. Each time she climbed back up in awe of the strength of a man who last night had been an incredibly gentle lover. With Parish Dunford you got so much more than what you saw, and the more she saw of him, the more she wished that wasn't the case. Because in less than forty-eight hours what Parish had given her would be well on its way to being nothing more than a memory.

For the last two days, they'd had Malagara to themselves, the other ringers having elected to spend their four days of R and R in Cloncurry, or the Curry as everyone seemed to call it, while Rusty and Leanne had taken the kids to visit friends in Mount Isa. Tomorrow night or early the next day, they'd be arriving back, and Malagara would return to work mode. She smiled, recalling the only time she'd sat down at the computer in the last couple of days had been to play an intergalactic war game with Parish. Naturally with her skill and experience she'd thrashed him on every occasion, but Parish was a good loser and very generous, not to men-

119

tion creative, when it came to giving congratulatory kisses to the victor.

She sighed. Something told her that once she left here, playing computer games wouldn't be the therapeutic outlet for her tension it had been in the past.

Two days. She and Parish had only two more days.

It occurred to her the commotion in the breaking yard had lessened, and emerging from her introspection, she was hit by a wave of pride at the sight of Parish now manoeuvring the horse with relative ease. The colt was still a long way from taking his defeat with benign acceptance, sulkily breaking from his gait every few strides, but it was evident his handsome rider had charge of the situation.

And he damn well knows it! Gina thought, grinning as Parish sent her a smug smile.

'Okay, I'm impressed! You can get down now,' she teased.

He shook his head. 'Five more minutes. This is only the second time he's had both me *and* a saddle on him. The first was the day before the last muster. I want to give him a bit longer to get used to it.'

'Okay. But is it safe for me to sit on the fence now and watch?' she asked.

'I'd rather you didn't. Just in case he suddenly takes it into his head to get ratty again.'

So Gina remained standing on the bottom rail of the fence, with her arms along the top one as a rest for her chin, listening to Parish's softly spoken words of encouragement to the young horse. Again she marvelled at the many and contrasting facets of the man. When it became obvious he was satisfied with what he'd accomplished and that she wasn't going to be required to radio the Flying Doctor to report he'd broken his leg, or worse—a thought she'd had more than once in the course of the last forty minutes—she returned to the house. It was her turn to cook.

She was busy preparing a salad when Parish opened the

screen door to enter the house, and just the sight of her stopped him in his tracks.

Her hair was loose around her shoulders, and backlit by the lowering sun shining through the kitchen's westerly window, it shone like a dark curtain of glossy black silk. She wore one of his cheap, unspectacular beige chambray shirts. The sleeves were rolled back into thick wads at her elbows, and the tail hung well past the middle of her thighs. From there stretchy black leggings took responsibility for her modesty. Her feet were bare.

There was nothing overtly sexy about her appearance or actions and especially not in the setting of the ancient kitchen, yet the overall effect was enough to rearrange his internal organs. Even allowing for the fact he knew he'd fallen head over heels for this woman, the force of his emotions staggered him.

Her head jerked up in response to the heartfelt groan he hadn't been able to contain. 'Sorry, sweetheart,' he said, letting the screen door slam behind him. 'I didn't mean to frighten you.'

'You didn't. Well, a little, maybe,' she amended.

Flicking her hair over her shoulder, she blessed him with a smile that immediately had him detouring from his automatic path to the fridge and kissing her. This woman's presence wasn't just powerful enough to override the habits of a lifetime. The sheer potency of the joy she created within him was addictive in itself. The taste, the feel of her, the way she moved against him, was something he couldn't get enough of, something that tempted him to push the limits of civility and good manners in his greedy thirst for satisfaction.

For long moments he feverishly plundered her mouth, hoping to draw enough sustenance from her sweetness to last him until he'd showered and was in a fit state to love her properly.

When Parish broke contact with her lips and started

drawing away from her, Gina instinctively tightened her
arms around his waist then proceeded to kiss her way over
his chin and down his neck to nuzzle her face against the
base of his throat. He smelled of horse and leather and
tasted of dust and sweat. She inhaled deeply, glorying in
the scented evidence of his hard work and raw masculinity.
The back of his shirt was damp beneath her fingers, and
she clutched at it, defying the male hands on her forearms
trying to ease her away.

'Ah, sweetheart, I'm all hot and sweaty,' he murmured
against her hair, then drew a long, audible breath. '*You*
smell so damn sweet and good...' He groaned. 'Gimme a
chance to have a shower and clean up.'

She shook her head, tilting it so she could look at him.
The action brought her hips into his lower body, the difference in height resulting in the hardness of his arousal
being pressed against her already sensually vulnerable
belly, where tiny sparks of white-hot heat were melting and
pooling into a warm wet puddle that threatened to drown
her from the inside.

'I don't want you cleaned up, Parish. I want you like
this.' Her eyes burned with a fierce, hot need that Parish
knew was mirrored in his own. 'Here,' she continued with
slow, throaty huskiness, her fingers working the buttons on
his shirt. 'Now. And *without*—' she stressed the word
through a smug smile, her deft fingers on his belt '—any
self-sacrificing nobility from you.'

And because Parish could deny her nothing, Gina got
exactly what she demanded.

In the removal of clothes, total nudity was disregarded
in favour of essentials only, desire outstripping traditional
protocol and primitive need overriding technique. Parish
still wore his jeans and boots when he collapsed on the
nearest chair and dragged a now buttonless-shirt-clad Gina
onto his lap.

In the rushed urgency of their passion, words came in

gasped, barely audible pants, making Gina wonder if the rate of her breathing was engaged in a furious race against the beat of her heart. Reality merged with fantasy, frustration with desire, as passion and emotions rose to possess not only her body, but her mind, too. Then, in the instant that Parish's body filled hers, she knew a moment of numbing, spiritual peace before she was again disoriented by the dizziness this man alone seemed to trigger.

She braced her palms against his shoulders in a feeble attempt to steady herself against the intoxicating sensations that battered her as Parish stroked one slow hand across her belly to close around her left hip and then used the other to cup and caress her breast. Even softer than his touch was his moan that told her her body's tremor of anticipation had been transmitted into and absorbed by his via the intimacy of their union. Or was it she who'd absorbed his? It was a heady and sensually powerful notion. She opened her eyes and met his, her breath catching at the awed tenderness reflected from their deep blue depths. The knowledge that it was directed at her seared her to the soul.

He pumped into her once, the action causing her to toss her head back with a throaty purr of pleasure. But cheated by his subsequent stillness, she frowned in puzzlement.

'No self-sacrificing nobility, remember?'

A broad, challenging smile widened his mouth as lust darkened his eyes. 'Ride me, sweetheart.'

For a moment Gina thought she'd fly apart from just the seductive tone of his demand, but mercifully she wasn't that far gone. Though she was a firm believer in the quality-over-quantity theory, in circumstances such as this, she wanted the quality to last for as long as possible!

The tiny lurch Gina's body gave in response to his words reverberated through Parish's body with erotic results. They were further heightened when she arched herself backwards and with an awkwardly outstretched hand snatched his dusty, upturned hat from the floor. Smiling seductively, she clamped it onto her head, then nestled herself firmly back onto him.

'I'm saddled up and ready to rodeo, cowboy…'

'C'mon, sleepyhead, up and at 'em!'

Gina levitated from the mattress at the unexpected smack on her butt. Though the Doona had prevented it from hurting, she didn't appreciate having her sleep disturbed.

'Rack off,' she mumbled, pulling the covers higher. 'It's still too dark to be anywhere near six o'clock.'

'Amazing!' he exclaimed, setting down the mug of coffee he held. 'You didn't even open your eyes and you could tell it was dark!' Her muffled response to that was probably as unprintable as it was unintelligible.

'I've brought coffee,' he continued in a cajoling tone, sitting on the edge of the mattress.

'I want sleep.'

'C'mon, don't be like that,' he whispered, leaning over to scatter butterfly kisses over her face. 'Half past five isn't so bad. It'll be six before you know it.'

She grunted, but with little conviction, as he pulled the covers down a little and kissed the tip of her exposed shoulder. Damn! But she smelled good! If he kept this up much longer he'd wind up climbing back under the blankets with her!

Giving her head a gentle stroke, he started to straighten. 'C'mon, sweetheart, you can't sleep the day away.' With cobra swiftness her arms locked around his neck.

'Why not?' she demanded, one eyebrow arched. 'You're making sure I'm not getting it at night.'

He rested his forehead on hers. 'Liar,' he whispered. 'You're getting plenty!'

'I meant *sleep*.'

'Can I help it if you're insatiable?' he asked, releasing her arms and holding the coffee mug to her.

'Yes. You're the one encouraging me,' she complained,

though her mouth was smiling when it met his to exchange a quick light kiss.

'So am I forgiven?' he asked eventually.

'That depends on the quality of your coffee.'

By Gina's preferred standards it was barely passable, but at least it was hot and strong. Lowering the mug from her lips she sighed appreciatively, although a lot of her pleasure came from viewing the muscled male back Parish displayed as he leaned over and pulled on his boots.

'Okay…you're forgiven,' she told him. 'For last night, at least. You're still not out of the woods for waking me this early. What's the deal?'

He sent a precocious wink over his shoulder as he crossed to the wardrobe. 'I've decided it's time to further educate you on how we do things in the country.'

She groaned. 'That sounds ominous. What do you have planned?'

He pulled his shirt on and proceeded to give his undivided attention to buttoning it. Her suspicious mind viewed it as an attempt at evasion rather than a sign his fine motor skills were giving him trouble.

'Parish?'

Innocent blue eyes lifted to hers. 'Mm?'

'What are you planning?'

He winked then started for the door. 'Get up, get dressed and find out,' he challenged.

Gina tossed a pillow at him, but he was out the door too fast and it landed benignly on the floor. 'You want to hope I'm not disappointed!' she yelled after him. 'Or you're dead meat, Parish Dunford!'

Male laughter from the hall was her only response.

'Okay, now you have a go,' he encouraged.

'No way, Parish!' she declared, stepping back and vehemently shaking her head. 'No way on earth! If I won't drink the stuff, there's no way I'm going to pump it!'

Shoving his hat back to expose more of his handsome, amused face, Parish rose from his crouched position to tower over her. 'C'mon, give it a try. It's easy.'

'I am *not* milking a cow, Parish. End of story.'

With one stride he'd closed the space between them and enclosed her in a bear hug. 'Hey, think of it as a once in a lifetime experience.'

'Having my appendix out was a once in a lifetime experience! So was losing my virginity and being electrocuted at fifteen. And believe me, none of those events left me with a taste for more once in lifetime deals, so you can forget the cow!'

He was staring at her with open fascination. 'You were electrocuted and lost your virginity at the same time?'

She blinked, momentarily sidetracked. 'What? No!' She rolled her eyes in exasperation. 'I was fifteen when I was electrocuted. I was nineteen when I lost my virginity.'

'How'd it happen?'

'I was in the back seat of a car—'

'No, you goose!' He laughed, giving her a gentle shake. 'I mean how did you come to get electrocuted?'

'As I started to say, I was in the back seat of a car...' She grinned at his bemused expression before continuing. 'A friend of mine was having a party, and when her dad went to get ice from the local self-serve garage we went with him. He put petrol in the car then went to the ice machine and got six plastic bags of the stuff. When he came out after paying he picked the bags up, three in each hand. Holding them by the necks of the bags, he started to carry them to the car. One dropped and burst open, so to save him having to put the rest down and get another one, I leapt out of the car and said I'd do it.'

She paused. She'd been asked to relate the story a thousand times, and her memory of the incident hadn't altered since the first time she'd told it.

'And?' Parish prodded gently.

'And next thing I know I'm lying in a hospital bed with my mother sobbing her way through the Hail Mary.' She shrugged. 'To this day that's all I remember. It was a stinking hot summer's day, and because the driveway was so hot, the ice had started melting the minute it was put to the ground. When the bag split, water trickled onto the adaptor joining the freezer lead to the extension cord, I stepped on it and got zapped. According to the doctors, all that saved me was the thick rubber surf thongs I was wearing.'

Parish hissed an obscenity and hugged her tighter. 'Lord, Gina! It's a miracle you weren't killed!'

Though she'd heard similar verbal reactions before, she was startled by Parish's ashen face and the tension gripping his body. Her story had really shaken him. She wrapped her arms around his waist and rested her head on his chest. Beneath her ear his heart was pounding. She felt touched by the depth of his concern for something that had happened to her so long ago, as well as guilty for distressing him.

'Does this mean you won't make me milk the cow?' she asked, hoping to tease him from his brooding.

It took a second, but to her relief a slow smile emerged on his face. 'Not in this lifetime or the next.'

'Good.' She rose on tiptoe to kiss him. 'In that I case, I'll go back and start getting breakfast while you finish with Clarabelle here.'

'Deal.' He released her. Then frowned. 'That's how you got those scars on the sole of your right foot, isn't it?'

She nodded. 'Part of the thong melted onto my skin. I can't believe you've been that observant of my feet. The scars are barely noticeable. They didn't even warrant plastic surgery.'

'I've committed every pore of your skin to memory, Gina. I know your body as well as I know my own.'

How ironic, she thought, turning towards the house, when she was beginning to think that until the last few days she'd never really known it. What's more, she was afraid she was getting way too fond of Parish's....

Parish watched as Gina peered warily into the creek. She wore a white one-piece swimsuit that hugged every lush curve of her body and contrasted temptingly with her smooth olive skin. And as luck would have it, the skimpy design left a lot of that skin on display. It was just as well he felt as if he could simply stand there all afternoon watching, because it was looking like that was all he'd be doing!

'Are you absolutely positive there are no crocodiles in here?' she asked. 'Because I've read all about those poor unsuspecting tourists who've been attacked.'

'Then you're definitely safe. You're far from unsuspecting Gina. That's the fifth time you've asked me that, and for the fifth time...there are no crocodiles this far south.'

'That's only reassuring if I believe crocodiles actually carry compasses!' she retorted. 'And if it's so safe, why aren't you in the water yet?'

'Because I thought I'd take the first shark watch.' The remark earned him a punch on the arm.

'I'm not *that* dumb!' she said haughtily. 'Oh, okay...I guess I can't put it off any longer. But—' she held a cautionary finger towards him '—if I end up main course for a croc, I'm going to haunt you until your dying day, Parish Dunford!'

Parish smiled. It was a hollow threat, since it was going to be the case anyway. It mightn't have been love at first sight, but the speed and intensity with which it had hit made up for the fact. Gina Petrocelli had entrenched herself firmly and permanently in his mind and heart for all time. He didn't know how Gina felt, and he was convinced she didn't, either. Which was why he hadn't admitted the depth of his feelings to her. Not because *he* was a coward, but because when it came to love he sensed Gina was. That she'd been burned once was blatantly obvious.

'I feel guilty, lying here,' she said much later as she lay stretched out on her back on a blanket. 'I should be in front of the computer working.' She turned her head to look at him. 'Correction, *you* should be in front of the computer and I should be standing over you teaching you how to use it.'

Parish traced a finger over one of her perfectly arched eyebrows, then let it trail down over her cheek, neck and finally under the strap of her swimsuit. Smiling, he slowly peeled it from her shoulder. 'But this is more fun. Don't you think?'

Helpless to do otherwise, Gina answered without words, and as he skilfully took possession of her mouth, her arm reached around his neck to make sure he didn't misinterpret her feelings.

Later, as she climbed into the passenger seat of the four-by-four for the drive to the house, she looked back at the crystal water and realized she'd felt less apprehensive about swimming with crocodiles than she did now. Because dry land or not, emotionally she felt like she was rapidly being swept out of her depth. Common sense told her it would be useless to try to swim against the current, but she didn't know how much longer she could tread water.

While the last three days with Parish had been the most wonderful of her life, they weren't indicative of her life. Or her.

She might have unexpectedly discovered she was good at wild, reckless lovemaking—correction! *sex*—but it wasn't something she could see herself indulging in long term. First because she seriously doubted her heart would stand the strain of that much physical exertion...and second, third, fourth and all the way to infinity, because she was beginning to suspect it would only be that way with Parish. Unfortunately Parish Dunford wasn't a long-term option for her.

Glancing at his strong workman's hands gripping the

steering wheel and his handsome face shadowed beneath his battered wide-brimmed Akubra caused her heart to do a funny little hiccup, and she felt the most ridiculous urge to cry. Fortunately, though, she was made of sterner stuff, and one good swallow dispelled the flash of silly sentimentality.

'Looks like Rusty and some of the boys are back a day early,' Parish said as they swung into the main yard of the homestead.

Gina followed his gaze to where a group of men stood inspecting a horse. The horse was a chestnut, but it was difficult to identify the faces of the men because of the tears blurring her vision. Whoever they were, their early return had cheated her out of a fourth and last glorious day alone with Parish!

'Yeah,' she said flatly. 'Looks like...'

CHAPTER TWELVE

WITH the sound of Parish's alarm clock echoing in her mind, Gina willed herself not to respond to the soft, light kiss he bestowed on the back of her neck. It wasn't easy. Not when her heart accelerated at the tenderness of his touch and her mind taunted her with remembrances of the passion they'd shared during the night.

Knowing they'd share no more nights together almost tempted her to give in to the urge to turn to him and press herself against his warm nakedness, but she realized that the end had to begin somewhere, and for the sake of her own sanity, it would start this morning.

Somehow she managed to imitate sleep even as he gently brushed her hair from her face and left a soft kiss on her temple. A moment later the mattress rolled as his weight lifted from it. Steadfastly she maintained her charade as she listened to the sounds of Parish dressing. Only when she was sure he'd left the room did she dare to open her eyes, and flipping onto her back she exhaled a long sigh.

In ten hours' time, he and the rest of the ringers would leave for the second muster, and it would be five weeks before they returned to Malagara. She'd be gone in less than two.

Her heart winced as sadness stabbed through her, but blinking until her vision cleared, she told herself to get used to it. There was nothing to be gained by deluding herself that cold-turkey withdrawal from the addictive sexuality Parish had introduced her to would be easy. She'd known all along there was a risk in experimenting with something she was genetically vulnerable to—raw, blue-collar masculinity—but she'd done it anyway.

There was a fine line between daring and stupidity, and she wasn't sure which side of it she'd been standing on when she'd chucked caution to the wind and leapt into a hot, torrid affair with a rugged stockman when urbane stockbrokers were more her style. Still, unlike her mother, at least she'd been aware of her susceptibility and not made the mistake of confusing lust with love. Therefore, she reasoned, giving up Parish Dunford wasn't going to be any more difficult than giving up smoking had been. Sure, it'd be hard, and there'd be times she'd probably crave the touch of his calloused hands and sweat-slicked body as desperately as she'd once craved nicotine, but she'd survive the discomfort and ultimately triumph over her addiction. If people actually died from not being able to get a fix of great sex, then the world would be seriously underpopulated!

'Well, my girl,' she murmured, tossing aside the covers. 'You've admitted you've got a problem, and as any counsellor will tell you, that means you're already on the way to a cure!'

She came into the kitchen fully dressed, but Parish forgave her the absence of her familiar sexy robe simply because the skin-tight jeans and sleeveless silk blouse she wore looked so damned good.

'Morning,' she said, smiling tightly and making a beeline towards the kettle for her usual caffeine hit.

'Good morning yourself. I was going to let you catch up on some sleep.' He winked. 'Since you've been blaming me for you not getting enough. Sleep, that is.'

She shrugged and turned away. 'I can catch up tonight.'

With smoothly efficient actions, she slipped two slices of bread into the toaster, then silenced the whistling kettle and poured its contents into her coffee mug.

'What's your schedule for today?' she asked, her attention on the cooking toast.

Parish was about to tell her they'd discussed this last night—he was going to be loading bullocks most of the day, and she was coming down to watch part of the procedure around lunchtime. But, knowing how testy she could be first thing in the morning, he decided to humour her. No sense walking into a dung pile you knew was there if you could go round it.

'The road trains are due down at the bullock paddock in about half an hour,' he said. 'If there are no hiccups, we should be done there a little after lunch. You want to ride down there or drive?'

'Neither. I'm not going.' She began buttering the toast with the concentration of a microsurgeon.

'Why not?'

'Because I don't want to, that's why.' Another of those short, curt smiles was directed his way. 'I can live without the experience of sitting around watching cattle loaded onto trucks. I've more important things to do. When will you be free?'

The quickly asked personal question negated some of his disappointment at the scathing tone she'd used, since it hinted that her edginess was due to the fact she resented the return to day-to-day work on Malagara because it would limit their time together.

'Reckon I'll be back about two. Three at the latest.' He eased back in his chair and folded his arms, knowing his grin went from one ear to the other. 'Got plans for me, have you?'

She averted her gaze. 'Yes. I want to run through some stuff with you. Today will be the last chance I get to go over the parts of the computer set-up you're still having problems with.'

Despite his best efforts to sidetrack her, Gina had been persistent and successful in getting him to spend a couple of hours each day learning how to use the program she'd installed. While he wasn't entirely ignorant of what computers were capable of and, thanks to his grandfather, had a solid understanding of bookkeeping, he'd been hard-pressed to keep his nose to the grindstone and his concentration focused on compiling data when Gina was within touching distance. All too often he found himself enthralled by the scent of her exotic perfume and the silky sound of her voice rather than what she was trying to explain or tell him to do. Today he knew he'd have no chance of managing it.

'What are you grinning at?' she demanded, after setting her mug and plate on the table and looking up to catch him watching her.

'The idea that you'll get me anywhere near that damn computer today. I leave on a five-week muster this evening. If you think that I'm going to waste time running my fingers over a keyboard when I could be running them over you, honey, you're crazy!'

'Parish!' she yelped as he hauled her into his lap.

'Ouch!' he yelped, as she freed herself with a well-aimed elbow to his sternum. 'Whatcha do that for?'

'Because I don't like being manhandled!'

'Since when?' He grinned. She didn't.

'Parish, it's time you started to take this computerization seriously. You're the one who asked to have it installed, you've got to be conversant with how it operates.'

'Why? I'll be *hiring* someone to do the bookkeeping come September, when I've got the mustering out of the way.'

'And who,' she demanded, tossing her hair over her shoulder as she took the seat opposite him, 'is going to teach them how to use the program, hm?'

He frowned, as much in reaction to the fact she'd shunned the seat beside him as to her question. 'Well, you, of course...who else?'

'Me?' She laughed. 'Parish, I'm going to be long gone

by September! In fact, I'm counting on being back in Sydney inside of two weeks.'

'What!' Shock had him on his feet. 'You're leaving?'

'Of course, I'm leaving.' Brown eyes flicked momentarily to his, then away. 'Once the program's up and running.'

'But you said inside two weeks.'

She nodded.

'But what about all the work you've still got to do? You said you needed herd figures and…and freight details before you could get everything set up. None of those'll be finalized until all the mustering is completed.'

'I don't need the final figures. You said that all musters are arranged identically and that the last step in the exercise is freighting the cattle to the saleyards, the abattoirs or down to Dunford Downs for fattening. Right?'

He gave her an absent nod, his mind still trying to come to terms with her blithe, totally unexpected announcement.

'So there you go!' she said, with pathetic brightness. 'After the stock is despatched today, it's only a matter of me working out the best way of incorporating the managerial and financial sides of that procedure into the program. Once I do, Malagara's computerization will be complete.'

'But there are still two more musters to go. Two *bigger* musters. What about all the information that'll have to be input or whatever you call it from those?'

Her eyes met his with impersonal directness. 'Any subsequent figures only need to be input using the same procedure as the first. It's simply a matter of repeating the procedure I've used. Naturally,' she went on, calmly lathering Vegemite on her toast, 'I'll leave detailed step-by-step instructions to follow, and print out a hard copy of all the necessary reports, so whoever inputs future data will have something to cross-reference and check their work against.'

'And what,' he asked, wondering if he'd ever wanted quite so desperately to shake a person, 'if they screw up?'

'They won't if they follow the instructions. And we have a phone support service, to deal with teething problems.'

Phone support! She was offering him phone support? What the hell was happening here? Had he slept through the alien invasion of her body during the night or was this some bizarre dream of his own?

'Don't look so worried, Parish.' Her tone was infuriatingly patronizing. 'If things are really desperate, a troubleshooter can be sent out to straighten things out.'

He latched onto the ray of hope. 'So you'll come back in September, if necessary?'

She nibbled at her mouth, her eyes not meeting his. 'No, not me. That's not part of my job. I *design* programs. Once they're up and running, I delegate any minor glitches to someone else.'

Parish felt as if he was going to explode. Anger, hurt and disbelief had risen to danger levels inside him. She was behaving as if she honestly expected him to be pleased with what she was saying.

'In other words,' he said, gritting his teeth, 'you get someone else to clean up after you.'

'No!' she snapped, giving him the satisfaction of at least having ruffled her oh-so-cool act.

'I take a lot of pride in my work. If I start a job, I make sure everything's running perfectly before I leave! I also endeavour to make sure the client or whoever's going to be using the program is competently conversant with how to use it beforehand. *Which*,' she stressed, 'is what I've been trying to do these last few days with you! *With*, I might add, minimum cooperation!'

'Well, guess what, Ms. Petrocelli—you're about to get even less! I'm out of here!'

'God damn it, Blue! You tryin' to start a stampede or what? I want the bloody beasts loaded *in* the cattle train, not scattered hell west and crooked!'

'Fair go, boss! I'm doing me best!'

'Hoy, Parish!' Rusty reined in beside him. 'You want me to take over running things?'

Parish glared at him. 'Why the hell would I want you to do that?' he demanded.

'To avoid a flamin' mutiny,' his friend said bluntly. 'You ride these blokes any 'arder and we won't have a ringer left on the place. Ease up,' he advised. 'They're doin' the job as well as any, an' better than most.'

Parish opened his mouth to argue then shut it. Rusty was right. He was taking his personal frustration out on the men. He sighed. 'Reckon I'm just edgy,' he muttered, not quite meeting Rusty's searching gaze.

'Yeah,' the other man responded. 'Like a cutthroat razor's edgy. You oughta go talk to Lee. She's about as happy as a feral bull in a rodeo chute, too.'

A small smile tugged at Parish's mouth. 'Always is when there's a muster starting and she's not going.'

'Yep,' Rusty agreed. 'That's *her* excuse. You got one?'

'I'm the boss. I don't need one.'

The redhead didn't flinch under the glare Parish nailed him with. 'If you say so.'

Parish stared at the star-speckled sky and told himself he had no reason to feel guilty for heading off without saying goodbye to her. She'd had plenty of opportunity to come out and wish them good luck, just as Snake and Leanne had before they'd left, but she'd remained in the house as stubbornly as she'd remained in the office while he'd been packing his gear.

'Guess a five-week muster ain't a big deal to a city slicker,' Blue had said in response to one of the many comments about her absence.

Parish had merely grunted, though he'd have given his new colt to know what the hell he'd done to trigger the outburst that followed his return from the bullock paddock.

Even now, six hours later, he was no closer to figuring it out.

Damn! He'd thought he was doing the right thing when he'd apologized and agreed to spend a half hour going over whatever she'd been so anxious to get done that morning. But no...

'I've decided there's no need to do that after all,' she'd told him when he'd got back to the house a little after two. 'It'll either be too little too late, or unnecessary.'

'This morning you seemed to think it vitally important,' he reminded her.

She'd shrugged. 'You're too preoccupied with the muster now to absorb anything new, and going over stuff you've already done when you've other things on your mind will only confuse you.'

'The only thing confusing me is *you*, Gina!' he'd retorted. 'How can you can go from being an eager and responsive lover one minute to being cold and indifferent the next?'

She'd not so much as flinched at his accusation. 'Parish, we both know I'm not indifferent to you.'

That had made him smile. 'I know, but you're trying damned hard to convince one of us you are.'

The clenching of her fists was the only indication he'd struck a nerve. 'Parish, we've had a wonderful four days together—'

'They're not over yet. I'm not due to leave for another two hours.' He'd reached for her then, grasping her wrist and drawing her to him for a kiss. For a moment, she'd kept her mouth firmly sealed, but he'd patiently taunted it into opening, and little by little her response had grown. Secure in her compliance, he'd lifted his head to gaze at her beautifully bemused expression. She'd looked so damn gorgeous it'd almost stopped his heart. The thought of five long weeks without her, of knowing he wouldn't be able to reach out at night and hold her was almost unbearable, and he'd told her so.

'I'm facing thirty-four long, lonely nights, but another two hours of this, of you, and the memory of it will just get me through—'

The unexpected force with which she'd shoved him away had caused him to stagger. Clearly he'd said the wrong thing, but she'd not given him a chance to ask what.

'We've made more than enough memories the last few days! I'm not interested in one more burning of the sheets for the road! Why is it with men like you sex is the first and last thing on your minds!'

'Men like me?'

'You come home,' she went on as if he hadn't spoken, her arms flailing in all directions, 'and you want to get laid. You're about to walk out the door and you want to get laid! You're all the same! Every last stinking one of you!' And with that furious and incomprehensible accusation she'd stormed into the office and slammed the door.

'So what the hell did I do?' he demanded of the stars.

'You using that reverse psychology again, boss?'

Parish glanced across to where Blue lay bundled in his sleeping bag. 'Nah, mate,' he said. 'I'm talking to the stars.'

'Uh-huh… Righto. Sorry to interrupt.'

'No problem, Blue.'

'Sure boss, if you say so.'

Parish had to fight down a chuckle at the man's less than reassured tone. The poor guy had had to endure his sleepless frustration the last time Gina'd denied him the opportunity to say goodbye by pretending she was asleep. And now this. The old ringer was probably beginning to think the boss was cracking up, which mightn't be too far from the truth. But one thing was certain, at this rate Blue wasn't going to be rushing to sign up for any more Dunford musters.

Sitting up violently, he swore. Damn it all! Blue was too good a stockman to loose!

Instantly he was out of his sleeping bag and tugging on his boots. In response to the urgency of his actions, Blue ricocheted into a sitting position.

'Problem, boss?'

'Yeah, but nothing you have to worry about,' Parish said quickly as the man started to unzip his own bag. 'I just realized I left the house without something important. I'm taking the white four-by-four. If I'm not back by morning, tell Rusty to head on to Number Three and I'll catch up with you there.'

'Will do, boss. Uh...what was it yer left without?'

Parish scooped up his saddle and sleeping bag in one go. 'An explanation.'

Parish knew the tinkle of his spurs had announced his arrival, but he said nothing as he hitched himself onto the railing of the seldom-used front veranda. There was no moon to speak of, and at ground level the stars were ineffectual against the thickness of the night. He waited until his eyes became accustomed to the darkness before turning his head towards the weathered rocker sitting halfway along the veranda.

She sat silhouetted against the shadows, her legs curled beneath her and her body angled away from him, so that her face was in profile. Parish reckoned a body-language expert would say she was trying to close herself off from her surroundings or something. He called it giving him the cold shoulder, and she'd been doing it long enough.

'You better tell me what I've done wrong,' he said, looking out at the blackened horizon. 'Because I'm usually pretty immune to sulking unless I know the reason behind it.'

It was a moment before she answered. 'I'm not sulking.'

'So why did you hole up in the office all afternoon and not come out until I'd left?'

'I was busy catching up on work.'

'That's rubbish, Gina,' he said calmly. 'And we both know it.'

She sighed. 'You're right. I was avoiding you. Satisfied?'

He felt like he'd been punched in the guts. 'Hardly. But at least you're being honest, so that's something, I reckon.'

'I've always been honest with you, Parish.'

'Bull. For four days your body's been telling me one thing and this morning your mouth starts trying to tell me something else.'

There was a stretch of dark silence before she responded. 'I'm sexually attracted to you, Parish. I've never denied that.'

'Nope! That's true enough,' he conceded glibly. 'In fact you've made it a point to ram home the fact my attraction is *only* sexual. I'm probably hard to please,' he said snidely. 'But I'd like to think if somebody asked you to suggest an epitaph for my headstone you'd do better than *Parish Dunford was a hell of a lay*!'

'Stop it!' she demanded, her head pivoting towards him. 'That's not fair, Parish! You're ruining what we shared! And I won't let you do that!'

'I'm ruining it! *I'm* ruining it?' A bitter laugh erupted from the pain in his chest. 'Oh, that's rich, Gina! That's really bloody priceless! Because you don't even *know* what we had! Hell, you don't even know I'm in love with you! And have been since the first time we made love. *Made love*, Gina!' he bellowed. 'Not *had sex*! Not *simultaneously climaxed* or any other of those bloody feminist terms and excuses you want to use! I *made love* to you, Gina, because *I love you*!'

The need to draw breath was all that halted his tirade. And except for his exaggerated breathing there was no sound in the inkiness of the night. Gina hadn't so much as moved at his declaration. Okay, so it wasn't the romantically delivered speech he'd intended, but surely to God she should've reacted to his shouting, if nothing else.

'Hell,' he said through gritted teeth. 'Aren't you going to say anything? Laugh, do *something*! At least acknowledge you heard what I said?'

'I…I heard.' Her voice was a tremulous whisper.

'And?' he prodded, fear and hope fighting for control of his heart.

'And…and…I love you, too, Parish…' He clutched at the timber upright to stop himself from falling as his body went limp with blessed relief. 'But it…it doesn't change anything.'

He laughed joyfully as he cut the distance between them and clasped her shoulders. 'The hell it doesn't!'

She shook her head. 'No, Parish. I'm still leaving.'

His grip tightened. 'In God's name, *why*?'

'Because,' she sobbed, her trembling hands cupping his face, 'your dreams are my nightmares.'

'Oh, sweetheart,' he whispered, gathering her close. 'I don't have the slightest idea what you're talking about, or why you're crying, but whatever it is we can work it out.' He pressed his mouth to the top of her head. 'I swear, honey, we'll work it out.'

Gina wished more than anything in the world that she could believe that, but she didn't. Shaking her head, she broke free of his arms, the immediate chill making her wrap her own around her. It didn't help, because the coldness she felt came from within, from her own despair.

'Gina…'

The confusion in his voice almost ripped her heart in two, though how that could be possible when it was already fragmented beyond repair, she didn't know. Unable to say what she had to while looking at him, she turned to stare blindly into the night.

'Parish, you told me that Malagara was your dream, even though you knew that the life would be a hard one.'

'Yes, so?' Impatience coated his words. 'You can be part of that dream, Gina. I want you to be. More than anything else.'

'But not more than the dream itself, Parish. Not enough to walk away from it.' She heard him curse under his breath and almost smiled, imagining the shocked expression he must be wearing. 'Relax,' she told him gently. 'I'm not asking you to do that, Parish. I don't believe people should sacrifice the essence of what they are on the altar of love.'

'The implication being,' he said, his voice terse, 'that's what I'd be asking you to do if I asked you to stay.'

'No, it's what I'd be asking of myself if I did,' she said softly, willing her voice to remain strong despite the tears burning her face. 'It'd be nice to believe that love conquered all, Parish, but I know from first-hand experience that it doesn't.'

Again there was a muttered masculine curse. 'You think that because some other bloke burned you real bad I'm going to do the same thing.'

'Not intentionally...' She paused to steady her voice. 'Unfortunately I'm the type to hold my hand over a flame. Which is why I've vowed not to play with matches.'

'God almighty, Gina!' Parish snapped, spinning her to face him. 'I love you! Will you quit talking crap and just give me the bottom line here!'

'The bottom line is...' She broke off as the temptation to simply fall into his arms threatened to overwhelm her. The need to let him make love to her one more time, knowing that he truly loved her, was nearly all-consuming. Nearly. But in her heart she knew that to experience that just once wouldn't be enough, and the need to repeat it would make it impossible for her to walk away. Ever.

'The bottom line is—' She drew a shaky breath. 'I love

you too much, Parish Dunford, to believe I'll be truly happy with you. I can't stay. Don't ask me again.'

Unable to bear the pain in his eyes or withhold the ragged cry that broke from her, Gina pulled free and ran into the house as unchecked tears rained down her face.

A few minutes later she heard the engine of the ute start up. That's when she really started to cry.

CHAPTER THIRTEEN

Six days later, Gina's bags were packed and standing by the bedroom door. Snake was going to drive her to the airstrip, and Parish had arranged for Ron Galbraith to fly her to Mount Isa for the flight to Sydney. Leanne had relayed this bit of information to her. Parish, not surprisingly, hadn't tried to contact her since he'd left her standing on the veranda that night.

Gina sighed and cast a last look around her room. Strangely, it didn't seem as Spartan as when she'd arrived. Well, actually it *did*, but for some reason she felt melancholy leaving it.

Some reason—yeah, right! she thought. And she wasn't melancholy—she was downright miserable! She threw herself onto the bed, so emotionally befuddled that she wasn't sure whether she should be ashamed or proud of the decision she'd made. Perhaps on a subconscious level she'd always known she was in love with Parish, but admitting it aloud had intensified her pain. Once voiced, it was that much harder to ignore, like a judge asking a jury to disregard an incriminating remark in a murder trial, which to Gina's way of thinking only reinforced the comment in the jurors' minds. She sure couldn't disregard the fact she'd admitted to loving Parish! And she'd *never* be able to forget that he'd said he loved her. 'Oh, God!' she muttered, covering her face. She wasn't going to cry again! She wasn't! She'd made her decision, and she'd made the right one!

'I did!' she said, punching the pillow. 'I did! I did!' She gasped as her tearful litany was interrupted by a memory. A loud memory. Certain she was imagining things, but stupidly hoping otherwise, she sat absolutely still, clutching the bedspread.

'Gina, this is Parish! If you're there, pick up!'

'Oh, Lord,' she whispered, still not moving. 'Parish…'

'Gina! Gina! For the love of God, if you hear me, pick up! We've got an emergency!'

Propelled by the desperation in his voice, she practically flew out to the C.B., her heart pounding so fast and hard it was as if she vibrated from the force.

'I'm here, Parish! I'm here!'

'Where's Leanne?'

In her scrambled state the question confused her. 'Leanne?'

'Yes! Where is she?'

The urgency in his voice frightened her. 'I don't know. Driving the kids to school, I guess. Parish, what— Wait a minute! She's pulling into her yard now. You want me to get her?' As she released the transmit button she heard Parish swear.

'Listen carefully, Gina. Rusty's had an accident. A real bad one. Get down to Leanne's right now. I don't want her on her own when she hears this. I'll give you time to reach her, then call again. Do it!' he barked. 'Now!'

Registering there wasn't time for questions, Gina dropped the handpiece and sprinted across the room. With an outstretched arm she flung the screen door open and tore through it, leaping down the steps of the veranda in one go. An unsteady landing reminded her of the high heels she wore. Without breaking stride, she reefed off one then the other, tossing them aside as she ran. Her haste gave her no time to think, to rationalize or to avoid the hard clumps of dirt that littered the four hundred metres to the Harrington house and bit into her feet at every stride. Ahead she saw Leanne pause in the act of taking Billy from his child restraint to stare at her. She ran faster.

'You wanna make the next Olympics or something?' the blonde teased when she reached hearing range.

There was a dull thud as the palms of her outstretched hands hit the side of the car as she used them for brakes and came to a panting halt. 'Parish just...called on the C.B.,' she gasped. 'There's been...an accident.'

All colour drained from Leanne's face. 'Oh, God, Rusty! It's Rusty, isn't it?'

Gina could only nod.

'Oh, God, no! What happened? Is he going to be all right?'

In the face of the other woman's panic, Gina struggled to stay calm. 'I...I don't know. I... Here, let me take...Billy for you and we'll go inside.' Lifting the sleeping toddler from the shell-shocked Leanne required nearly all of what little strength she had left. *How long had she been so out of condition?*

Dismissing the irrelevant thought, she called to the small girl wandering away from the house. 'Kaylee! Kaylee, honey, come inside.'

'I'm not Kaylee! I'm Kellee!'

Sucking in yet another long breath, she hiked the sleeping boy higher on her hip. 'Whatever,' she said. 'Get inside anyway.'

With rolling eyes the child started to obey. Leanne, though, was still rooted to the spot next to her car. Gently Gina took hold of her forearm and guided her towards the house.

'What...what's happened?' Again the question was whispered, Leanne's eyes glazed in confusion and disbelief as she frowned into Gina's face.

'I...I'm not sure. But Parish is going to call back. Leanne, wait!'

By the time she hurried into the house, Leanne was already trying to get a response on the C.B.

'They're not answering! Damn it, why isn't someone manning the bloody thing!' she demanded.

'Leanne, listen to me. You've got to calm down. You'll frighten the kids.' Gina added the last simply because it was the only reason she could think of. *Why the hell wasn't someone manning the C.B. on the other end?* Where was Parish? Why wasn't he—

Dear Lord, was it possible he was hurt, too? Her heart and lungs iced over. Fear rose like bile in her throat. Thankfully, the weight in her arms moved and dragged her mind from the brink of something too painful to consider. Something she wouldn't consider. Parish was okay. He had to be.

'Leanne, why don't you put Billy in bed?' The woman's glazed eyes wavered between her son and the radio, then back again. 'C'mon,' she urged. 'It'll only take a second. If I do it I'll probably wake him. You'll hear the C.B. the instant anything comes through.'

Finally Leanne moved to take the sleeping child from her. 'It's serious, you know,' she said, her face solemn with certainty. 'Otherwise, Parish would've called me first.'

Gina couldn't deny the comment, but confirming it outright seemed too cruel. 'Would he have been able to get you in the car?'

Immediately Leanne's expression brightened. 'No! No, the C.B. in my car's been taken out for repairs. Oh, Gina, maybe it's not so bad. Maybe it's only a broken arm or leg?'

Gina forced a smile. 'Let's hope so.'

She watched in dread as Leanne left the room somewhat appeased. *Oh, Parish*, she thought, *if a broken leg doesn't qualify as a major concern...how bad is real bad in your world?*

Unfortunately, she found out all too soon. Less than a minute later, his static-rough voice intruded into the room. After establishing Gina's presence, he addressed Leanne.

Listening as he gave details of how Rusty had been thrown headfirst into a tree and knocked unconscious when his horse stumbled at speed, Gina was achingly aware of the suppressed emotion in his tightly controlled voice. These two people were his closest friends. She could only imagine how he must feel. She closed her eyes in the vain hope she could telepathically offer him some comfort.

'Leanne,' he said thickly. 'He's regained consciousness, but…but…' He swore violently before continuing. 'Lee, it looks like he's suffered spinal damage. He's got no feeling from the neck down.'

The handpiece fell slackly from Leanne's hand. 'No! Oh, Lord, no!'

The agonized denial caused the room to tilt, and the consoling grip Gina had on the other woman's shoulders tightened to become a support for her own knees. How ironic that she could feel so much pain when Rusty, hurt and broken, could feel none.

'Oh, Rusty! No! No!' Though Leanne's denial wasn't transmitted, Parish's response was further evidence of how close he was to these two people.

'Leanne, honey, listen to me. The one thing Rusty doesn't want is for you to fall apart. I know—by God I know—what you're feeling, but he's counting on you to hang in there. Leanne? Talk to me, kiddo.'

Blinking back her tears, Gina stroked the lowered head of the hopelessly sobbing woman and picked up the handpiece. 'It's me, Parish. Leanne can't talk right now.'

'How is she?'

She sucked in a long, steadying breath before answering. 'As you'd expect. Is there anything I can do?'

'Just stay with her till Snake gets there. I contacted him out at the Tea Party bore. He was coming in after lunch to drive you out to the airstrip, but I've told him to head back now.' He sighed wearily. 'I don't want Leanne left alone until we get some official medical diagnosis on Rusty. If that hasn't come through by the time you have to meet Galbraith's pilot at the airstrip, drive yourself down there and have Snake stay with Lee. We can pick the vehicle up later.'

The thought of leaving had never entered her mind, and she was angry that Parish would assume it had under the circumstances. Did he really think she was the type to just walk away from a crisis like this? For a man who'd claimed he was in love with her, he sure didn't seem to have too high an opinion of her! But now wasn't the time for righteous indignation.

'Ask him what's happening with Rusty,' Leanne urged, lifting her tear-stained face.

Nodding, Gina depressed the transmit button. 'Leanne wants to know what's going on?'

'We've contacted the Flying Doctor base at the Isa. They're organizing a helicopter—there's no way they'll get a plane in where Rusty is. The chopper will take him to the airstrip on Marks Downs, since it's closer than ours. A plane and medical team will meet it there.'

Leanne snatched the radio from Gina. 'Go with him, Parish!' she demanded. 'I can't get out there in time, so I want you with him! I don't want him to be alone.'

'I know you don't, honey, but it mightn't be possible for me to go. It'll depend on the size of the chopper. But I promise he'll get the best medical attention available. I swear, I'll make sure he gets the very best. But if there's room I'll go with him, okay?'

Gina felt a momentary lessening of the tension in Leanne's shoulders at Parish's words.

'Listen, Leanne,' he continued. 'I want to get back to Rusty. Blue's here now, so I'll leave him to man the radio. Any messages you want delivered?'

Fresh tears swam in Leanne's eyes. 'Just tell him I love him.'

'Guess what?' Parish returned softly. 'That's exactly

what he said to tell you. That and not to worry. Now how about you get Gina to fix you a cup of tea and go lie down, okay?'

Though she'd nodded agreement when Parish had made that suggestion, the closest Leanne came to complying with it was to sit nervously on the edge of the sofa watching the tea go cold. Gina's heart ached for the woman, and she hated her inability to be able to offer any comments that didn't sound like the useless platitudes they were. In the city she could've bundled Leanne into the car and driven to whatever hospital Rusty was being taken to and met the ambulance. At least then she'd have felt they were doing something. Out here they could only wait for the next bit of news.

During the next thirty minutes Gina made another pot of tea, endeavoured to keep Kellee subdued enough not to wake the sleeping Billy and did her best to offer what positive support she could to Leanne, who seemed to be becoming more and more agitated. Every few minutes she got up to prowl aimlessly around the room before fingering the loudly silent radio and commenting, *'They'll call as soon as they have news,'* before drifting back to the sofa and gingerly lowering her pregnant frame onto it. The intensity of her distress was evident in every line on her face and in the eerie tonelessness of her voice as her conversation jumped from continued verbalizing of her disbelief at what had happened to recalling past incidents of her and Rusty's life together.

When Billy awoke with a wail, Gina felt a wave of irritation at the shift in the status quo, then guilt that her feelings must have shown when Leanne sent her a rueful grimace and announced that she'd go change him.

'No, no. You stay put,' Gina said quickly. 'I'll do it.'

'Do you know how?' Leanne sounded doubtful. 'I don't use disposable nappies.'

No, Gina thought, that'd make it too easy! 'I'll manage.

C'mon, Karlee, you can show me where your mum keeps everything.'

The little girl looked up from the modelling clay she was playing with wearing an impatient frown. 'I told you, I'm Kellee.'

'Right. Sorry. Well, come help me anyway.'

It took Gina a good fifteen minutes to complete the task, but not because of her inexperience or the little boy's penchant for wriggling and squirming. Kellee's idea of helping would've qualified as industrial espionage in the computer industry! However, what little satisfaction and triumph Gina was feeling when she returned to the living room vanished the instant she saw the contorted face of the children's mother.

'*Leanne, what is it*?' she asked, racing to the woman's side even as she wondered how she'd failed to hear the C.B. 'What's happened? Why didn't you call me?'

Leanne drew a long, unsteady breath before answering, her eyes wide with terror. '*I'm having contractions.*' She grabbed Gina's shoulders and shook them with frenzied force. 'My God, Gina, I *can't* go into labour now! I simply can't!'

If Leanne hadn't been holding her, Gina was certain she'd have slumped to the floor.

'You heard anything yet?' Snake demanded the moment he raced through the back door.

'Thank God you're here!' Gina had never been so glad to see anyone in her life.

'How's Rusty? Where's Lee?'

'Last we heard they were waiting on the Flying Doctor.'

The old ringer muttered under his breath as he scanned the room. 'Where's Leanne? Is she holdin' up okay?'

'Not really. She's gone into labour.'

'What! You mean she's havin' the baby?'

Gina figured Snake's look of horrified disbelief was

probably an exact replica of what her own must have been when Leanne had broken the news. She nodded.

'She's havin' the kid *now*? *You're* gonna deliver a baby?'

Gina's stomach rolled at the thought. 'I take it you're not volunteering?'

'Hell, I can't do it! I'm a mechanic!'

That Snake's protest was registered on job demarcation lines rather than sexual ones made Gina smile, but the man in question clearly didn't. He looked positively panic-stricken, which meant he was in sync with her and Leanne on that score. She only hoped that when she told him what his part in the game plan was, he wouldn't bolt for the door.

'Snake,' she said, keeping her tone calm and in control. 'The contractions are about two minutes apart. Now I've already spoken with the Flying Doctor base,' she told him. 'And here's what we have to do...'

'Righto, girls,' Gina said, entering the dining room and addressing the four children sitting listlessly around the table. 'Billy's finally asleep. So let's not breathe too loudly for the rest of the night, eh?'

The teasing comment didn't draw even the tiniest of smiles from the normally rowdy Harrington children. Not that Gina was surprised or that she felt much like smiling herself. She'd thought she was doing the right thing when she'd insisted on picking the three eldest girls up from the property where they attended school rather than letting them sleep over as the owner had suggested. Kellee had cried inconsolably for her sisters once Leanne had left, so getting the girls had seemed the best move. Besides, Gina had always believed that families should be together in a crisis, and this was certainly a crisis. The last report they'd had on Rusty was that he was being transferred from Townsville hospital, where he'd originally been taken because of his possible head injuries, to the spinal unit at

Brisbane's Princess Alexandra hospital. He was conscious, but still paralysed from the neck down.

Becoming conscious of an unpleasant odour, she pulled the wet front of her blouse away from her skin. Changing nappies on little boys was an experience full of unexpected surprises. With a sigh she tucked a loose strand of damp hair behind her ear. She was going to have to either change into something of Leanne's or trek up to the main house and unpack something, but first she had to get the girls settled. Or as settled as she could under the circumstances.

'Okay, now I've got Billy down, I think the rest of us ought to start getting ready to pack it in, too.'

'You said we could call the hospital and check on Mum again.' Kylee reminded her defensively.

'And you can. But the hospital isn't going to appreciate us phoning every half hour, so let's wait a while.'

'No! I want to talk to Mummy! I want to talk to Mummy now!'

'Oh, Kellee, I know you do, sweetie. But the hospital won't let you.' Gina went to hug the four-year-old, but the child pushed her away.

'You sent her away! You sent my mummy away!'

Kellee's tearful accusation was the same one she'd been making all afternoon. Gina was too tired to defend herself again. She could only be grateful that Snake had managed to get Leanne to the airstrip without having to play mid-wife, and that Ron Galbraith's pilot hadn't cracked when he'd had to fly a pregnant passenger in labour to Mount Isa rather than the computer programmer he'd been expecting.

'Can't we call the hospital where Daddy is and talk to *him*?' Kaylee asked. 'At least that might shut *her* up.'

'No!'

'Well, geez! You don't have to bite her head off!' Kylee retorted, 'It was only a suggestion.'

Gina didn't mean to snap, but at Leanne's request she

hadn't yet mentioned anything to the girls about Rusty's spinal injuries, and she didn't want to run the risk of them finding out. Not yet.

'You're right, Kylee. I'm sorry, Kaylee. But I think it's best to wait before we ring either hospital again. The longer we wait,' she said, trying to sound positive, 'the more good news they'll have to give us.'

'Can't we call Parish?' Karlee asked.

'No need, I'm here.'

Gina pivoted around to meet the full impact of Parish's questioning gaze. There were too many emotions assaulting her senses for her to name even one. It had been the day hell rejected, but now Parish was here. The cavalry had arrived, and she could relax enough to breathe again. How ironic that just this morning this man had been the sole source of her anguished emotions, and now he was the solution to them. She was so relieved just by his presence her eyes blurred, and her first instinct was to throw herself into his arms, but the children had beaten her to him, so instead she slumped onto the nearest chair before her knees could give way.

She propped an elbow on the table, rested her forehead on her hand, closed her eyes and drew several long, calming breaths. Parish could handle things now. He could deal with the petty sibling fights brought on by wrought nerves and uncertainty. He could decide how much or how little the children should be told about the condition of their father. He could try to break past the hospitals' standard line—'The patient is doing as well as can be expected'—and get a straight answer to the question, 'Are they improving?' He could worry about whether Snake's prolonged absence meant that the man's departure to get 'one drink to calm the nerves' had escalated into a couple of bottles. Parish could take responsibility for everything. Especially the children. Gina didn't want to be solely responsible for the wellbeing of the Harrington children. For any children. Not again.

Little by little, the sound of the male voice gently comforting, reassuring and responding to the myriad of questions and fears the girls tossed up penetrated her brain, drawing her attention to the scene around her.

Parish was crouched down, holding a four-year-old on one knee and a sobbing seven-year-old in the other. The two older girls stood to either side, their hands on his shoulders, listening to his every word. Gina understood their need to establish physical contact, for Parish Dunford had an aura of inner strength, stability and competence that made a person feel everything would be all right simply because of his presence. She sighed. Competence, stability and fortitude were traits she'd spent half her life trying to develop and the rest of it believing she'd succeeded. Yet her time at Malagara had shown her that in reality her confidence and control were little more than a well-rehearsed act.

It was then she realized that for all his patience and kindness to the girls, Parish looked even more emotionally and physically fatigued than she felt. It was utterly selfish of her to be luxuriating in self-pity and buck passing when he looked only a heartbeat away from complete exhaustion. Determined to make amends, she quickly hurried into the kitchen.

Caught up in the babbled confusion of the girls' chatter and still off balance from the events of the day, not to mention his surprise at finding Gina still at Malagara, Parish was caught unawares when a cold beer was shoved into his hand.

'C'mon, you pair, let Parish have a beer,' Gina said, decisively taking the youngest girl from his arms. 'I've run a bath for you. Kylee and Kaylee,' she went on over the top of the younger pair's complaints about taking the tub, 'start clearing the table. I've turned the spaghetti bolognese on to reheat. When it's hot, dish some up for Parish and make a fresh pot of tea.'

'Okay,' Kaylee said, as Kylee headed towards the table without comment.

Unsure whether he was more bemused by the parental authority in Gina's voice or twelve-year-old Kylee's docile obedience, he set Karlee on her feet. 'Uh-uh, you heard Gina,' he said when she refused to let go of his neck. 'Go have a bath and get ready for bed.'

'Will you tuck me in, Parish? *Please*? Since Mummy and Daddy aren't here?'

Averting his eyes from the child's watery ones, he looked straight into Gina's. They, too, were overly bright, and it was only the knowledge that surrendering to the urge to haul her into his arms this minute would further tighten the emotional ropes currently threatening to strangle everyone that stopped him from doing so.

'We'll talk later,' she said, as if reading his mind. 'The kids need to get to bed.'

Looking into the forlorn, seven-year-old face of the child holding on to him, he gave her a reassuring squeeze. ''Course I'll tuck you in, princess.' He kissed her forehead. 'Call me when you're ready.'

It was almost forty minutes before Gina reappeared, by which time Parish had finished his beer and a second serving of spaghetti and was helping the older girls do the dishes. He didn't think he'd ever seen anyone looking quite so lost, so uncertain of what she was expected to do. Yet from what Kylee and Kaylee had told him it was obvious she'd coped remarkably well.

'Parish?' she said, tentatively. 'The little ones want you to tuck them in.'

'Well, that's good to hear. You've been gone so long we were beginning to think you'd all drowned. Or were making sure you missed out having to help with the dishes.'

Though normally the teasing comment would've been

harmless, given the circumstances Gina thought Parish's choice of words was clumsy, at best. She cast a quick, concerned glance at the two youngsters standing beside him only to find they were actually smiling.

'Parish phoned both the hospitals,' Kylee told her. 'They've stopped Mum's labour.'

'That's terrific!' Gina exclaimed, instinctively elated until she realized that nothing had been said about Rusty's condition.

'And Dad's doing as well as can be expected,' the girl continued. 'Not that *that* tells us anything.'

'It tells you all you need to know, so go have your baths,' Parish said, sending Gina a quick glance and a minuscule shake of his head. 'Isn't that right, Gina?'

'Yeah, that's right.' Forcing a smile, she reached for the kettle. 'You girls hit the bathroom. I'm going to get myself a caffeine fix. You want a cup of tea, Parish?'

The lack of a response had her turning towards him, to find him watching her with a strange expression that seemed to be a blend of confusion, pleasure and abject disappointment. Then he smiled—that soft, gentle smile that had a way of making her feel as if it had momentarily righted all the world's wrongs.

'Sure,' he said. 'Take it out on the veranda when it's ready, I'll be out shortly.'

CHAPTER FOURTEEN

GINA was studying the satellite tower adjacent to the house, vital to the Harrington kids being able to do something as mundane as watch TV, wondering why a woman would chose to raise a family in such an isolated region. How could Leanne even think of having a baby this far from a state-of-the-art hospital?

She didn't react when she heard the screen door open and the tinkle of spurs as booted feet moved to the table, where she'd left a cup of coffee and a plate of chocolate biscuits. Or rather, she didn't turn around. Inevitably her heart went into that funny little skip pattern it always did whenever Parish was around. Love. That was the cause. She knew it. As surely as she knew there was no medication available to correct the irregularity in the vital organ, just as she knew that the events of today had once again highlighted the futility of that love and the satellite dish reinforced the message.

From where she sat on the bottom step, she turned to look into the face of the man who stood towering above her. The glow from the kitchen light inside the house wasn't bright enough to reveal his expression, and the overhang of the veranda roof blocked the moon.

'You were holding something back when you told the girls the hospital said he was doing as well as can be expected.'

'The last message Snake gave Blue was that Leanne didn't want anyone telling the girls about the paralysis.'

'She didn't.' Gina wasn't sure if this was wise or not, but initially she'd been grateful that Leanne's decision had spared her the responsibility of having to break the news to the girls. Yet when Snake had abandoned ship, leaving her alone with the five distraught kids, she'd felt as if she was being criminally dishonest every time she opened her mouth.

'It hasn't been easy keeping it from them,' she admitted aloud. 'It's not so bad when I'm on the phone to the hospitals, but every time someone calls on the C.B. to enquire about him or pass on their best wishes, I'm terrified they'll blurt it out. It's like trying to walk barefoot through crushed glass.'

The contact of Parish's body against hers as he lowered himself onto the step beside her immediately nullified the chill breeze. It seemed like a lifetime since she'd been close enough to feel his body heat, smell the earthy masculine scent that was uniquely him. Never had anything been so reassuring.

'Well, maybe you won't have to worry about that much longer. The good news is Rusty's got the feeling back in his legs. The doctors think it'll only be a matter of time before he regains it in his upper body, too.'

'Oh thank God! Oh, Parish! That's wonderful!'

Perhaps it was only genuine delight that spontaneously propelled Gina into his arms, but Parish didn't care. All that mattered was that she was where he needed her to be. Just being able to hold her again seemed like the greatest favour God could've bestowed on him. He drew her closer, tightening his arms around her, sending up a silent prayer of thanks as her arms immediately reciprocated.

'Oh, Parish...Parish, I was *so* scared,' she whispered brokenly against his neck. 'I didn't know what to do when Leanne went into labour. The baby isn't due for another two and a half months! We're nearly three hundred kilometres from the nearest hospital!' Her words were rushed and fervent. 'Leanne was all het up. She was crying about Rusty, about the kids, getting more and more upset about everything. Billy and Kellee were crying. When I tried to get through to you, Blue said you were on your way to the hospital in Townsville with Rusty. Snake wasn't back. Oh, God, Parish, I thought I'd have to deliver the baby!'

She jerked her head back to look at him, her eyes bright with tears. 'I couldn't have done it,' she told him earnestly. 'I'd have thrown up. I know it. Or fainted! And even if I hadn't, the baby would've died. It was way too early! People aren't supposed to have premmie babies out here! It's insane to live out here! There's no neonatal facilities. No specialists or doctors. The Flying Doctor base had all their planes already out. Snake said even the nearest *vet* was more than a hundred and twenty kilometres away! He actually suggested we get some ringer off some nearby station to come over because he'd heard the guy once did a Caesarean on a horse! A *horse*, for God's sake!'

Parish smothered her words by pulling her against him. He knew she wouldn't appreciate seeing him smiling when she was so genuinely upset, but he couldn't help it. He loved it that his cool, confident career girl had a marshmallow heart and a vulnerability that she let only him see.

'Shh, sweetheart,' he said, stroking her back and the silkiness of her hair. 'Shh. You did great, honey. Better than great. Leanne's labour's been stopped, Rusty's improved. It's gonna be okay, sweetheart. Everything's going to be all right.'

He continued to utter the soft reassurances, matching his words to the rhythm of his hands as he stroked her shoulders and back. And knowing he was responsible for being able to bring about the gradual decrease in tension in Gina's body wrought the same therapeutic release in his own. This woman's happiness was intrinsically linked with his own, and he needed her in his life.

'You know,' he said sometime later, shifting so his back was supported by one of the veranda's timber uprights and Gina was snuggled into the valley between his bent knees, her cheek resting on his chest, 'I didn't expect you to still be here. When I got the message Lee was in labour and Galbraith was going to fly her into the Isa, I assumed you'd go with her.'

'I thought you were in Townsville.'

'The message about Lee came through as we were about to get on the plane. I decided to head back, knowing Snake wouldn't be able to manage the two little ones.' He frowned, recalling he'd radioed his intentions to Blue and told him to pass them on. 'Snake should have told you that.'

'I haven't sighted Snake since I came back from driving over to pick up the kids from school. I can't *believe* Leanne drives that distance twice a day!' she added. 'Anyway when I finally got back here, there was a scrawled note saying Rusty was on his way to Townsville hospital and Mount Isa hospital was still trying to stop Leanne's labour. And he'd gone to the stockmen's quarters to shower and have a drink to calm himself!' There was more than a little irritation in her voice. 'He'll be permanently calm if I get my hands on him any time soon!'

Parish laughed. 'Relax. I radioed the muster camp while you were bathing the kids. Apparently, old Snake figured it was the time for all good men, et cetera, and he's on his way out there to help out with the mustering.'

Her head came up from his chest. 'Help out with the mustering! If I asked him to so much as bring Leanne a glass of water or do something with the kids, he acted as if it was brain surgery and started muttering about how he's *only a mechanic*!'

'Yeah, well, I reckon Snake feels mustering a mob of wild cattle is a safer sideline than mustering a mob of wild kids. Besides, he probably felt you had everything well under control.'

'Ha! He didn't stick around long enough to find out!' She sighed heavily. 'I've been at my wits' end.'

'Not according to what the kids have told me. Or,' Parish said, 'what I've seen since I got here. Not too many single women could've handled five distraught kids and organized things as well as you seem to have done. And I doubt Leanne finds time to cook spaghetti sauce from scratch even on a good day. Actually, Gina Petrocelli, I'd say that for someone who professes to being not cut out for motherhood, you have a natural talent for it.'

'Then you'd be wrong. It's not natural talent I have, it's experience.'

For a moment Parish thought he'd misheard her, but the stiffness of her body and the tightness of her voice told him otherwise.

'Years of experience at changing and feeding babies, of bathing and picking up after kids, of wiping their tears and reading them stories and putting them to bed. But you know,' she said, 'all that practice doesn't make it perfect. Not for me, anyway.'

Disbelief, amazement, denial and God knows how many other sensations clogged his numb brain. *She was a mother? She had a child? Children?* A thousand questions fought for the right to be asked first, but in the end all Parish could do was voice his generic confusion.

'I…I don't understand what you're saying.'

With a muttered curse, Gina let go of him and ran an aggrieved hand through her hair. 'God, I don't even understand it,' she said, tipping her head back as if she really was addressing heaven. 'Even after all this time, as much as I love my family, a part of me still resents them for that part of my life.'

'Gina, are you going to tell me now, after all this time, that you have children?'

'No. I'm going to tell you why I don't want to have them.'

The crisp clarity of her response seemed to drop the temperature twenty degrees. Yet when she spoke again, her voice was faint and detached as if was coming from far, far away, and though she still sat within touching distance, the way her arms embraced herself and her gaze was fixed on the dark horizon, Parish knew she was emotionally beyond his reach.

'I've only got vague memories of my life up until I started school, but I think I'd probably lived in about a hundred small country towns by then. My father was a shearer, and we moved about to be near where he was working,' she explained. 'But he always seemed to be away from home. He was when I started school, because I can remember being all dressed up in my uniform and Mum crying because her darling Pete couldn't see how grown up their little girl was.'

She gave a bitter laugh. 'Darling Pete didn't give two hoots about their little girl. All my father ever cared about, on the rare occasions he was home, was that there was food and beer in the refrigerator and that Mum didn't spend all her time fussing with me and ignoring him. Which of course she didn't, because she was hopelessly in love with him. Whenever he left she'd just sit for hours crying and crying and telling me how much she loved him.'

'Like I said, we moved around a lot, following my father's work, but that's not to say we saw him regularly. Sometimes he'd go off and we wouldn't even *hear* from him for months, but Mum always talked about him like she was expecting him home any minute, and this time he'd decide to stay. He never did,' she said flatly.

'Some people remember major events in history by where they were or what they were doing at the time. I pretty much calculate how frequently my father put in an appearance in my life by counting back nine months from the births of my sisters. I was seven when Mum had Carmen and ten when the twins were born. My father wasn't around to see any of them as babies or at too many stages after that. Basically his total input into our lives was the contribution of his sperm at conception and his name on a birth certificate. His catch cry was he needed his freedom. Mum and welfare payments raised us.

'I love my mother. I *know* she did her best for us during those years, but God, I'm still so angry at her for her stupidity where my father was concerned! Whenever he was around nothing and no one else existed for her. It didn't matter that he'd get drunk and abusive with her or that there were other women when he was away. The minute he walked into the house and said, 'Has my best girl missed me?' she was in his arms, his bed and his total control. She'd succumb to his good looks and rugged macho charm as easily as she breathed. There wasn't anything she wouldn't and didn't do for that selfish, sweet-talking bastard.'

Seeing the source of the *'men like you are all the same!'* tirade the other day, Parish was tempted to launch into a defence of himself, but she didn't give him the chance.

'He got into debt somewhere over in Western Australia and wrote and told Mum that if he didn't pay it he'd end up in gaol. Even at ten I knew that was the best thing that could happen to us, but not Mum. No, she went out and got a job as a cleaner in a motel so she could get a loan to help him out. Then she got a second job at night, pumping petrol at a service station, so she could offset what it cost her to pay someone to look after the kids until I got home from school.'

'Until you got home from school?' Shock fostered Parish's interruption. 'But you were only ten! Just a little girl.'

'Oh, no, Parish, I was *a hundred and ten*. I'd become a big girl once Carmen came along. Who do you think cooked, cleaned and cared for the little ones when my father was home and Mum was falling over herself to be at his beck and call?

'No, Parish,' she said. 'Mum going to work merely meant that I had to do it all the time. I was the one who took Carmen and the twins to school on their first days and the one who stayed home when they were sick. I was the one who had to stay up until Mum came home of a night and tell her what was going on in our lives, what the dentist had said, what the plumber had said, what things the kids needed for school.' She paused and drew a long, audible breath. 'And I was the one who four long, unbearably hard years later had to tell her that the man she loved more than anyone or anything on earth had been killed in a pub brawl.'

The crude four-letter word Parish spat was mild compared to the outrage he felt at what this woman had endured in her childhood. Yet at the same time the intensity of her pain didn't make venting his rage a priority. First and foremost the hurt, the guilt, the fear currently shadowing the most beautiful face God had ever created had to be erased.

When he reached for her, she came easily into his arms and snuggled urgently against his chest.

'She was heartbroken by his death,' Gina went on. 'I wanted to slap her for crying, Parish. Because, so help me God...' Her voice broke. 'I was glad, actually glad. I hated that life! I don't want that responsibility again! Never!'

'Ssh... It's okay. Don't talk any more.'

Against his chest she shook her head. 'I...I want to tell you. I need to tell you all of it or you'll only get half the picture.'

It was only as she spoke the words that Gina realized exactly how true that was. At twenty-eight her life fell into two fourteen-year periods so completely different that an account of only one of them could in no way explain the person she was today. From nightmare to fairytale.

'While my mother was working at the motel, she became friendly with one of the regular guests. He was a wealthy Italian involved in real estate and working on a local development. Since they were the only Italians in town, Mum invited him to a traditional Italian dinner one Sunday, and after a while it got to be a regular thing. As far as my mother was concerned they were only friends, but Anthony Petrocelli wanted it to be much more—'

'Petrocelli?' Parish interrupted, sounding stunned. 'The Anthony Petrocelli of the ten richest men in Australia list?'

'Yep, that's him. Dad was slotted in at number seven on last count, I think.'

'Dad? I thought—'

'My natural father was Australian. His name was Peter Henley. But as far as I'm concerned, Tony Petrocelli is the only dad I've ever had. He married my mother ten months after Peter was killed, and he adopted us girls. He's been a kind and loving father and a wonderful husband to my mother for the last fourteen years, and if he could erase the previous fourteen he would. For himself as well as me,' she said sadly.

'You sound like you feel sorry for him.'

'I do. He adores my mother, but he also knows that even though she loves him, he wasn't and never will be the love of her life.' She sighed. 'I asked him once if that bothered him, and he said not really, because it meant that even if he did inadvertently hurt her it could never cause her the same depth of pain my father had.

'Anyway,' she said, her tone lightening as she continued, 'needless to say, going from a life of pretty much abject poverty into one of servants, private schools and overseas vacations was quite a turnaround for a fourteen-year-old girl. For the first time in my life I had a social life and nice clothes. Money wasn't a problem, no matter what I wanted. I got a horse and riding lessons for my fifteenth birthday, my own personal telephone line and credit card with a fif-teen-thousand-dollar limit for my sixteenth, a sports car for my eighteenth and a penthouse apartment for my twenty-first.'

A wry smile tugged at her mouth. 'But the most valuable thing Anthony Petrocelli gave me was personal freedom.

He liberated me from having to feel responsible for anyone but myself. I can't tell you how great that felt, Parish. It was...it was like being able to *breathe* for the first time, like having been chained up for years and then being released.' She threw her head back and laughed. 'Oh, Lord, it was wonderful! *Is* wonderful. I'm twenty-eight years old and I can do anything I want to do, go anywhere I want to go. The only obligations I have are those I *choose* to have, like my career. Having children would seriously change all that.'

Her voice sobered, and when she looked at him her brown eyes were steady as they held his. 'I know that sounds selfish to a lot of people, but in my opinion the most essential qualification for being a parent is being someone who isn't afraid to take on the responsibility of others. And the bottom line is, *I am*.'

'I think,' Parish said, 'that the most essential quality it takes to be a good parent is the ability to give love unconditionally.'

She shook her head. 'My mother loved Peter Henley unconditionally, and look what happened. You can't rely only on love to guide your decisions in life. Especially not where kids are concerned. Parenting is too hard a job, one I've already had experience of. And I'm in no hurry to go through that again. Not for anyone.'

'I see.'

Gina had never known pain as sharp or all-consuming as that inflicted by the resigned acceptance in Parish's words. It was intensified when his large, calloused palm rose to caress the side of her face.

'I love you more than I ever imagined loving anyone, Gina,' he told her. 'When I came in and found you still here, I thought, *Second chance, Dunford! Convince her to stay. Do whatever it takes to keep her here.* I told myself I was going to make love to you until the thought of leaving me would be incomprehensible to you.' A lopsided, ironically sad smile tugged at his mouth. 'And I could do it, couldn't I?'

'No, I—' She broke off, her fingers gripping the front of his shirt and twisting in the fabric. With a defeated sigh, she closed her eyes, then nodded. Two tears slipped beneath her lashes and rolled down her cheeks until Parish leaned forward and caught them on his tongue. Instantly she moaned, using her hold on his shirt to draw him nearer as she twisted her face to place her mouth beneath his. For one long, blissful minute, Parish allowed himself the luxury of tasting her before pulling back. Tangling his fists in her hair, he held her head level with his, tightening his hold just until she opened her eyes and met his.

'I do want to make love to you tonight, Gina. Tonight and every other night for as long as you're here, but only because I need you and want you and know I'll never get enough of you. Not because I want to manipulate you into staying. I love you, Gina, and I know you love me, but I promise you I'll never use that love to hold you against your wishes. You're free to leave whenever you want. Or to stay as long as you want. No pressure, no strings...and no responsibilities.'

'Oh, Parish.' She shook her head ruefully, her mouth smiling even as a solitary tear slipped from her too bright eyes and her hands rubbed against his unshaved jaw. 'Why the hell couldn't you have been a city stockbroker instead of an Outback stockman?'

Parish could have told her that it wouldn't have made a difference. That the major stumbling block to them having a future together wasn't the differences in their lifestyles or her fear of being accountable to or for someone else, or even her reluctance to have children. No, their problem was that Gina Petrocelli was scared to death of being in love. Because it was a fear she had to recognize and overcome on her own if she was ever going to be completely cured, Parish didn't say anything. Instead, he simply brought her mouth to his and silently vowed to love her as best she'd let him for as long as she'd let him.

the room where the kids slept. I thought maybe you'd be
staying around a while longer.'

Gina believed in the women's grapevine read from ear to
Parish, for both of them. 'Oh, er, no. I've got a job and I...'

'Gina's leaving on the same flight and stays in the
next day or so,' Parish cut in, not looking in her direction,

CHAPTER FIFTEEN

Two days later, Gina stepped into the airconditioned terminal of Mount Isa airport wondering how the day had
come to pass so quickly.

It had been barely dawn when Parish had reluctantly
called a halt to a night of the sweetest loving she'd ever
known to hustle her into the shower so they could start
getting the five Harrington kids ready for the trip into
Mount Isa hospital to see their mother before they flew
back to Brisbane with one of Leanne's aunts.

Though the doctors had succeeded in holding Leanne's
labour at bay, she'd been told to take things very easy for
the next ten weeks if she wanted to carry her baby safely
to full term. With five kids and the school holidays starting
next week, she'd planned on getting her aunt to come and
stay at Malagara, but since Rusty was still in Brisbane's
Princess Alexandra hospital, with the aunt's agreement
Parish had arranged a more satisfactory plan.

He organized a charter plane to fly the woman to Mount
Isa to see Leanne, pick up the kids and fly back to Brisbane.
In a week's time, once Leanne was discharged, she'd be
flown by air ambulance to join them, which meant she'd
be near Rusty and be able to see him daily.

'Oh, Parish,' Leanne had said, wiping away tears of happiness. 'I don't know how to thank you. Me and Rusty...
Oh, God, we're just so damn grateful to you for what
you've done. I'm so sorry all this had to happen smack in
the middle of mustering.'

'Good. Then don't do it again.'

She'd laughed and nodded, then looked at Gina, her eyes
taking in the tailored navy business suit. 'So you're leaving,

eh? From what the kids said, I thought maybe you'd be sticking around a while longer.'

Gina blushed as the woman's gaze flicked from her to Parish, then back again. 'Um, er, no. I've got a job and...'

'Gina's wardrobe is a bit limited for long stays in this neck of the woods,' Parish said, coming to her rescue with a grin and a wink. 'But I've managed to pin her down to a visit once we've got the mustering out of the way.'

'Good.' Leanne nodded. 'In that case we'll schedule the christening to coincide with it.' A smile spread over her face. 'Can't have a christening without a godmother, can we?'

Gina had been stunned. 'A god—oh, really, Leanne, surely there's someone else you'd rather—' She'd broken off in the face of the other woman's shaking head.

'It's my way of thanking you for everything you did that day and for taking care of the kids. Please say yes.'

Gina had found herself having to swallow to keep her tears at bay as she'd nodded her acceptance.

'We've got a bit of time to kill.' Parish intruded into her thoughts, indicating the departure schedule. 'Why don't we check your luggage and then go get something to eat,' he suggested. 'I don't know about you, but I loathe airline food.'

So did Gina. Nearly as much as she loathed the strained, plastic, polite, clichéd conversations people used when they weren't sure what they should say.

All in all, it had been a day full of sentiment and un-checked feelings, from the kids' tearful reunion with their mother, the hugs and kisses they'd bestowed on Gina as they'd boarded their chartered flight, to Leanne's insistence she be the baby's godmother. Somehow she'd managed to keep the events from rubbing against the rawness of her emotions, but now, when Parish was looking everywhere but at her, as he recited a long list of complaints about meals he'd had while flying, Gina felt her control slipping.

She knew she wouldn't be able to endure the remaining seventy minutes to boarding time alone with him without dissolving into tears. *Like she cared about the similarities between inflight chicken and rubber*!

'No,' she heard herself say. 'I don't want you to wait.'

As she'd expected, her announcement immediately halted both his words and the progress of the luggage trolley he was wheeling towards the ticketing counter. Straightening, he shoved his hat back on his head to stare at her with his penetrating blue eyes.

'Tell me why not.'

'You know why not.'

'Tell me anyway.' The request was pitched low and gentle, touching her soul and causing tears to well in her eyes. She blinked, sending them onto her cheeks.

Parish silently cursed himself as Gina lowered her head and unsuccessfully tried to hold back a sob. Damn! What was the matter with him? He'd vowed not to use emotional blackmail against her, and yet that's exactly what he was doing! Uncaring of where they were, he pulled her into his arms and kissed her as if his life depended on it. It did. The trouble was she wouldn't allow herself to feel the same way, didn't want to feel the same way.

'I'm sorry, honey,' he said, nuzzling her neck. 'That wasn't fair. If it's going to be easier for you, I'll go. C'mon, let's get your stuff booked through—'

'No!' Her arms tightened around his waist.

Hope rose in his chest until it nearly choked him. 'No?'

'Not yet. Wait. I want you to hold me for a little longer.'

Disappointment replaced the hope, ripping out his heart. For a moment he didn't trust himself to speak and buried his face in the silkiness of her dark hair, trying to remind himself that her happiness was ultimately paramount to his own.

'Sure, sweetheart,' he said finally. 'I'll hold you for as long as you want.'

The truth was, he wanted to hold her for a lifetime. The fantasy was hearing her ask him for forever. The reality was walking out of the airport terminal exactly eighteen minutes later...alone.

Gina was totally oblivious to her fellow passengers as she sat in the departure lounge, staring at her boarding pass. If this was what she wanted to do, why couldn't she stop crying? Sure, she'd expected to be unhappy about leaving, but what she felt was a million times worse than unhappy.

Which was ridiculous, she told herself, because it wasn't as if they'd just ended everything cold, like they had before the crisis at Malagara had given them a second chance. *They were going to maintain their relationship.* They'd phone each other and take vacations together, even spend the odd weekend together when their work schedules permitted. It wasn't over, it was just going to be different, that was all.

Parish had said he'd stay at the house tonight so she could phone and let him know she'd got home safely, and though he wouldn't be able to phone her while he was off mustering, he'd call her as soon as he got back. She'd hoped he would be able to fly to Sydney for a few days when the ringers took their break before starting the final muster out at the Long Way Camp, but she should've realized that with Rusty being hurt, Parish couldn't afford the time off.

Still, he is *going to call you,* she reminded herself positively, and it wasn't that long until November, when she'd be able to take a week or so off and come up to Malagara. Six months wasn't a long time. Not really. She'd thought four weeks seemed like a long time when she'd first got up here, and look how fast that had gone. *Too fast.* The time seemed to have flown. But then she'd been with Parish.

Even when he'd been away on a muster she'd still been

surrounded by evidence of his presence. The scratched coffee table in front of the sofa where he'd laze back and prop up his feet before he realized he still had his spurs on. The sight of his shaving gear in the bathroom, the beer cans cooling on the bottom shelf of the refrigerator in readiness for when he came home at the end of a long, sweaty day. And of course it had been impossible to sit in the office and not remember the first time he'd made love to her, impossible not to feel her heartbeat pick up or recall the scent of sweat and seduction in the air and the excitement of his touch.

Yes, at Malagara, Parish Dunford had been a part of her life even when he wasn't actively in it, and it wouldn't be any different in Sydney, not really. Oh, sure, she'd have a limitless supply of hot water, wall-to-wall carpet and every modern appliance a woman could wish for, but she wouldn't have Parish. She wouldn't have sex without a safety net.

You and Parish don't have sex, you make love! she quickly chided herself. What they shared was the most wonderful, exciting, stop-your-heart-and-steal-your-breath love any two people could! The most incredibly beautiful, sensual and spiritual love on earth. And it would always be like that for them, even if their relationship was only a part-time one. Even if—

'Oh, my God!' Gina yelped, jerking out of her slouched position on the chair. *'Oh, God, no!'*

She didn't care that her discreet sobs had escalated and she was drawing the attention of those around her. *Let them look*, she thought, pulling yet another tissue from the second of the two purse-sized packs she'd purchased only minutes earlier. It was pretty pointless trying to save her public face when she deserved the title of fool of the century!

'You are so stupid, Gina Petrocelli,' she muttered. 'Stupid, stupid, stupid!' She'd been so obsessed with not repeating her mother's mistakes that she was on the verge of duplicating her father's. Of treating the precious gift of deep, one-of-a-kind love like a part-time hobby!

By the time her flight was called she'd calmed down enough to get to her feet. Her eyes felt puffy and her head ached, but aspirin would cure that quickly enough. Unfortunately, though, it wouldn't help a broken heart or terminal idiocy. Taking a deep breath, she slung her leather designer backpack onto one shoulder and without another moment's thought screwed up her boarding pass and headed for the exit.

'Stupid,' she repeated. 'Really, really stupid!'

Sitting on the veranda in the stillness of the crisply clear night, Parish heard the sound of the unfamiliar engine long before it came into sight and the direction from which it came told him it wasn't one of the station vehicles coming in from the muster.

Remaining seated, he tried to guess who was likely to be calling in at ten-fifteen at night. If he got lucky, the approaching car might be a couple of ringers who'd heard of Rusty's accident on the bush telegraph and come to Malagara on the off-chance of picking up some work. When he'd checked in with Blue a couple of hours ago to let him know he'd be back in the saddle tomorrow and to ask if he wanted anything specific brought out to the camp, that had been at the top of the bloke's wish list—more ringers. Apparently in the three days he and Rusty had been away, what was to have been five weeks of hard work had rapidly started to resemble seven weeks of hell.

'Well, Blue,' he said aloud, getting to his feet when the vehicle came into the main yard. 'Looks like you struck out.' No one who regularly drove around this part of the world was going to do it in a tiny four-cylinder job like the one that stopped a few metres away.

Standing at the top of the steps, he waited for the driver

to kill the headlights that were all but blinding him and get out. 'Something I can do for you?' he asked loudly when neither thing happened and he was forced to shield his eyes.

'Can you forgive me for being an idiot?'

Parish froze, unable to believe the voice he heard came from the car and not his imagination. Then the headlights went off, the door opened and Gina climbed out to stand behind it.

'Failing that,' she said, 'could you at least give me a cup of coffee before you send me packing again? I brought my own coffee percolator and some real milk.' There was a hint of nervousness in her voice and the way she clasped the top of the open door. The car's interior light was sufficient to show she'd traded the suit she'd worn earlier for jeans and a denim jacket.

'Planning on staying a while, are you?'

'That depends on whether stupidity has been made a criminal offence. If it has, then I'm public enemy number one and the cops will probably be here any minute. Actually, given my record they'll probably re-introduce the death penalty for me.'

'I see.'

'I thought, since this place is so isolated, you might let me hole up here for, say, oh, fifty or sixty years.'

Parish's heart nearly exploded through his chest. 'That long, huh? Sounds like you're more or less volunteering for a life sentence anyway.'

'I am,' she responded solemnly, standing absolutely still.

The urge to just leap off the veranda and drag her into the house was almost overwhelming, but he restrained himself. The decision to come this far had been all her own, and he wanted the last few steps to be motivated solely by what she felt for him, not what he could make her feel.

'It's a tough, isolated life out here,' he continued, playing devil's advocate. 'A city person could get pretty miserable after a while.'

'Maybe,' she conceded, looking around at the vast silent landscape surrounding them, before stepping away from the car and slamming the door. 'But the city can be tough and isolated, too. Especially if your thoughts and your heart are constantly somewhere else.'

Not taking her eyes from his, she began to slowly walk towards him. 'Misery isn't entirely geographically based,' she said, stopping at the bottom of the stairs.

Parish's heart was drumming so loudly he was convinced it had jumped into his head and taken up residence next to his brain.

'I love you, Parish. I'm always going to love you, whether I'm here or in Sydney. Maybe there will be times when life out here gets me down, but you'll at least be close at hand. In Sydney you wouldn't be.' Smiling wryly, she negotiated the first step. 'I guess the bottom line is... I'd rather be miserable with you than without you. I—'

Parish caught her mid stumble.

'Damn! *When* are you going to fix that step?'

Grinning, he pushed her hair from her face. 'I'm not sure. I never can seem to get around to it.'

'Then I'll ask Snake to do it...after he installs the new hot-water tank that's being delivered next week, that is.'

'You've arranged to have a new hot-water tank delivered?' he asked, bemused.

'Yes. I mean, if I'm going to be out here for fifty or so—'

As his mouth closed over hers, Gina was certain she felt her future shift from badly off-centre to perfect. Never in her life had she felt so secure or certain of who she was and what she wanted and who she could be.

The creak of the floorboards as they walked down the hall and into the bedroom was like music to her ears. Who needed plush wall-to-wall carpeting? she thought. And where was the attraction in a white on white bedroom and a waterbed if Parish wasn't the man with her? she asked herself as he lowered her onto his standard mattress, kissing her at the same time.

'New clothes,' he observed, when they quickly began undressing each other. 'And not a designer name in sight.'

'My luggage was already on the plane,' she told him as they started unbuckling each other's belts. 'And even a city slicker like me knows you can't go to a muster camp in a suit.'

Parish's hands instantly stilled. 'You plan on coming out to the muster camp?'

Though he sounded startled, Gina heard the underlying pleasure in his words.

'I don't just want to share your dream, Parish, I want to help make it come true. I mightn't know much about the life on a cattle station yet,' she said. 'But I'm tough, I can ride and I'm a quick learner. I'm not the type to sit at home wringing my hands, wondering if you've been hurt and praying for you to walk in the door.'

Her voice was earnest, but her attention and hands stayed on the task of undressing him as she spoke.

'I intend to learn everything about the cattle business, and wherever it takes you, I'm going to be right alongside you every step of the way. Not because I have to, but because I want to be.' Her thumb grazed his mouth. 'Always.'

The sincerity in her words both touched and frightened him. Easing back on his knees, he brought her into a sitting position, supporting her back with one arm and using his free hand to hold her chin so he could see her face. As always, her beauty momentarily distracted him, her lips luring him into a long, tender kiss before he spoke.

'I love you, Gina. I'm not your father, and I swear you don't have to be afraid I'm going to flit in and out of your life the way he did to your mother's. There's not a chance in hell of that ever happening.'

'I know that, Parish.' She surprised him by grinning. 'But even if I did have my doubts, it couldn't happen, be-

cause I'm not my mother, and there's not a chance in hell
I'd let it!'

In that instant, Parish's last lingering doubts vanished.
This incredible woman was just as committed to ensuring
she was a part of the rest of his life as he was.

'Do you have any idea how much I love you, Gina
Petrocelli?' he asked, pushing her onto the mattress.

She smiled. 'Yes. But show me anyway.'

'I intend to.'

Their remaining clothes and further conversation were
rapidly dispensed with, and as Gina lay naked in Parish's
arms her sole thought was to reveal her love to him with
as much physical eloquence as he was using in displaying
his to her.

Every touch of his hands or mouth against her body was
a delicious blend of tenderness, protectiveness and the type
of arrogant male possessiveness liberated women publicly
rejected in the name of political correctness but privately
craved in their carnal fantasies. Yet because she'd finally
allowed her heart its ultimate freedom, and no longer feeling the need to ride shotgun on it, it added an extra di-
mension to their lovemaking. And Gina found herself hurt-
ling towards an emotional climax at the same speed as she
was a physical one.

When Parish's mouth suckled her breast, she felt not
merely the tightening sensation deep in her womb, but a
contraction in her heart at the thought that if she wanted it,
this man's seed could produce a life in that womb. A life
that would rely on her breasts not for pleasure, but for
comfort and sustenance. Together she and Parish could produce another human being. The thought was as dizzily
powerful as the physical sensations Parish created in her
blood. She clutched at his shoulder in an attempt to steady
her mind, but the ripple of muscle beneath her fingers defeated the effort by tempting her to explore him further.
When she did, she discovered he was sheened in sweat and

took erotic delight in tasting the salty wetness of his flesh and gliding her hands across the smooth, slick surface, then along the ridges of his spine until he shuddered in response.

Though it was impossible not to feel feminine smugness at the effect she had on this man, at the same time Gina found it emotionally poignant knowing that these same muscles had developed as Parish raised another kind of sweat in the hard, physical pursuit of his dream. A dream he had loved her enough to offer to share with her.

'Gina, honey...open your eyes.'

His request made her smile. In the philosophical sense, her eyes were already open. Never had she seen or felt anything more clearly. But she obliged nonetheless, her breath catching at the depth of love shining from eyes as blue as the Outback sky.

'It's different, this time,' he whispered, his hand lifting in slow motion to caress her cheek. 'You feel it, too.'

Gina could only nod and blink against the tears that suddenly blurred his handsome face. He eased back until he was straddling her, his knees taking the bulk of his weight while his inner thighs embraced her hips and his arousal brushed provocatively against her. Impatiently she wriggled to bring him nearer...deeper.

'One second, honey,' he said thickly. Without taking his gaze from her face, he interlocked the fingers of his right hand with her left, then his left with her right, before resting them on either side of her head. Every action was deliberate and executed with innate gentleness.

'Look at me,' he commanded softly. And as she did, he entered her in one long, smooth stroke that filled her with a sensation she could only describe as *all things good*.

In that millisecond of time, Gina read a vow of endless love, trust and faith in his eyes, and as her heart soared, she returned it with her own.

The intensity of their emotional commitment acted to send their physical one over the edge, and Parish's clenched jaw showed the strain of his fight for control as he moved against her.

'I'm not sure how long we can make this last, honey,' he gasped raggedly.

'Forever,' she whispered, arching against him as she reached an arm up to pull his head towards hers. 'Forever and ever and ever...'

EPILOGUE

SITTING on the veranda, Gina took one look at her four-year-old daughter's grubby face, torn T-shirt and dusty jeans as she rode on her father's shoulders, and felt her heart explode with pride and happiness.

The last six years of her life had been more wonderful than she could ever have imagined possible, and not a day passed when she didn't thank God that she'd come to her senses and learned to trust her heart's judgment.

It was three days shy of what would be her sixth mustering season, and the changes to Malagara were almost as sweeping as those in her outlook on love, life and all it entailed. The original house had been modernized and redesigned almost beyond recognition, and although it didn't have anything as impractical as white carpet, it did have airconditioning, a TV and an unlimited supply of hot water. They also had a plane, which Parish had insisted Gina learn to fly so she could escape to civilization whenever she felt the urge. She rarely did.

'Looks like someone will be needing a bubble bath before dinner,' she said, standing as Parish carried their daughter up the solid sandstone steps of the veranda. 'Madeline Louise Dunford, how on earth did you get so filthy?'

'I was playing with GinaLee,' the blue-eyed brunette responded. Though a part of her still cringed at the name, it had been her goddaughter, GinaLee Harrington, who'd ignited Gina's maternal instincts.

'It involved Barbie dolls and large amounts of mud. See?' Parish winked and lowered his daughter to the ground. 'I told you I'd watch her and help Snake with the pump at the same time.'

As her daughter ran and bestowed an enthusiastic hug and kiss on her, Gina thought she'd overdose on the blessed purity of her love.

'Can I go ask Judy to run my bath now?' her daughter asked excitedly. That was another change at Malagara. They now had a housekeeper, since most of Gina's time was devoted to either parenting, working alongside Parish or doing the accounts. Parish stubbornly maintained he could only use the computer to combat aliens.

'Sure, sweetheart,' she said. 'Tell Judy I'll be in shortly to wash you.'

Parish grabbed her from behind and nuzzled her neck. 'Maddy's not the only one who's filthy,' he said, doing delicious things to her ear with his tongue. 'You going to wash me, too?'

'Mmm. Maybe later.' She turned around in his arms and began nibbling on the exposed flesh of his throat. His skin had the scent and taste of hard work and excited her as it always had. 'It depends.'

'On what?' he asked, trailing his mouth down her neck and his hands onto her buttocks to draw her closer.

'On whether you promise to return the favour.'

'Done.' He groaned, bringing his mouth to hers for a long, deeply satisfying kiss. The fact he could ignite her to passion with next to no effort was one of the few things that hadn't changed on Malagara and they broke apart reluctantly, knowing that passion couldn't be fully satisfied until after their daughter was in bed. As far as Gina was concerned, that was the only downside to parenthood!

'I thought she looked really tired,' Parish said with a wry smile. 'I think we should put her to bed early. After all, she'll have a big day tomorrow, with the new ringers arriving.'

Gina laughed. 'You're incorrigible.'

'That the same as insatiable?'

'In your case, yes!'

They walked arm in arm into the house, but when Gina would've continued straight to the bathroom and Maddy, Parish veered in the direction of the kitchen. She smiled to herself as he made a beeline to the refrigerator, opened it and reached inside to snag a can of beer from beside a two-litre plastic container of milk.

Those were two other things that hadn't changed in six years—Parish still liked a beer when he got in from working, and Gina still wouldn't drink or pump cow's milk!

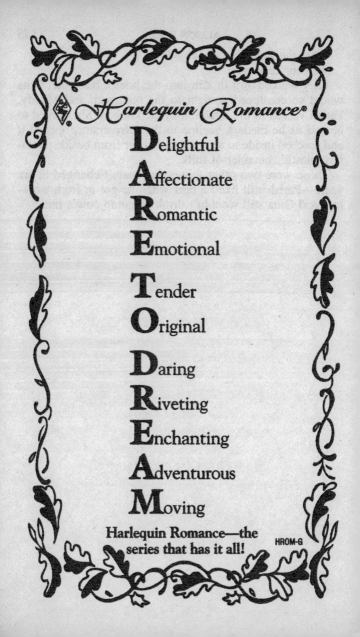

Harlequin Romance®

Delightful

Affectionate

Romantic

Emotional

Tender

Original

Daring

Riveting

Enchanting

Adventurous

Moving

Harlequin Romance—the
series that has it all!

HROM-G

HARLEQUIN PRESENTS®

HARLEQUIN PRESENTS
men you won't be able to resist
falling in love with...

HARLEQUIN PRESENTS
women who have feelings
just like your own...

HARLEQUIN PRESENTS
powerful passion in
exotic international settings...

HARLEQUIN PRESENTS
intense, dramatic stories that will keep you
turning to the very last page...

HARLEQUIN PRESENTS
The world's bestselling romance series!

Harlequin® Historical

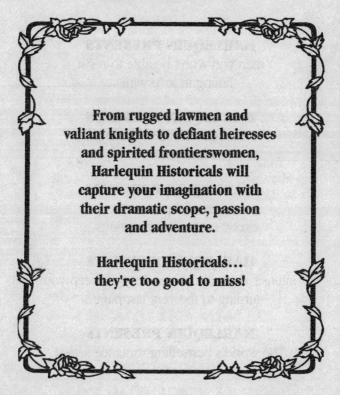

From rugged lawmen and
valiant knights to defiant heiresses
and spirited frontierswomen,
Harlequin Historicals will
capture your imagination with
their dramatic scope, passion
and adventure.

Harlequin Historicals…
they're too good to miss!

LOOK FOR OUR FOUR FABULOUS MEN!

Each month some of today's bestselling authors bring
four new fabulous men to Harlequin American Romance.
Whether they're rebel ranchers, millionaire power brokers
or sexy single dads, they're all gallant princes—and
they're all ready to sweep you into lighthearted fantasies
and contemporary fairy tales where anything is possible
and where all your dreams come true!

You don't even have to make a wish...
Harlequin American Romance will grant your every desire!

Look for Harlequin American Romance
wherever Harlequin books are sold!

HARLEQUIN SUPERROMANCE®

...there's more to the story!

Superromance. A *big* satisfying read about unforget-
table characters. Each month we offer
four very different stories that range from family
drama to adventure and mystery, from highly emotional stories to romantic comedies—and
much more! Stories about people you'll
believe in and care about. Stories too
compelling to put down....

Our authors are among today's *best* romance writ-
ers. You'll find familiar names and
talented newcomers. Many of them are
award winners—and you'll see why!

If you want the biggest and best
in romance fiction, you'll get it
from Superromance!

Available wherever Harlequin books are sold.

Look us up on-line at: http://www.romance.net

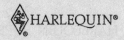

Not The Same Old Story!

 Exciting, glamorous romance stories that take readers around the world.

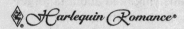 Sparkling, fresh and tender love stories that bring you pure romance.

 Bold and adventurous—Temptation is strong women, bad boys, great sex!

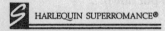 Provocative and realistic stories that celebrate life and love.

 Contemporary fairy tales—where anything is possible and where dreams come true.

 Heart-stopping, suspenseful adventures that combine the best of romance and mystery.

 Humorous and romantic stories that capture the lighter side of love.